# Smallpox Hill

George Fane

Copyright © 2016 George Fane

All rights reserved.

ISBN: 1536841234
ISBN-13: 978-1536841237

For Rachel

# CHAPTER ONE

The second time I meet Paul, he is trying to buy a door for a very dented Mercedes from a car wrecker down on the Bristol Road. This is early May.

Paul is about forty. He is balding but his head is shaved. He isn't very tall and he isn't very fat. He is tanned but he isn't glamorous. He is genial, smiles a lot and also has some barbed sense of presence, as though, if we dig sufficiently deep, we will come across the real sharp Paul, the ruthless and hard part. Even now though, on this second meeting, I know I like him, for some reason that I can't put my finger on. Is there a chemistry in emotion, like people say. a well disguised one, that we aren't consciously aware of?

So - as he squeezes my hand and I try not to catch his eye – although I know I like him, I don't know that he'll take up a lot of my time, this man. Instead I stare at his face and lips.

There are moments, odd ill-defined moments, that, if we had just known, even the faintest touch of clairvoyance, then we would act differently.

But we don't and life goes on.

As he squeezes my hand this is one of those moments and instead of concentrating, I look up at the silver birch just coming into leaf and see how the tiny leaves play with the light in the way that they do.

"How you doing, Doc?" he says. He smiles, does Paul, in a haphazard way, like a leer, nearly. Like he wants something.

I have to say I hate it when people call me doc. I see myself as easy going and tolerant but some things just get to me. I think maybe that it's a creeping Americanisation, this doc business, as though I'm in some western, with Gin slings and guns being slung around. Or maybe it's a term of faint derision. I'm not exactly sure. I am, after all, just a country doctor, the wrong side of thirty living out my life of low stress and slight underachievement, trying to care for people but not get too involved. This is the west of England, where the land tips into Wales. But there, the western bit ends. I have never seen a gun in my life, not yet anyway. And though there has been maybe too much gin, I am just trying, like everyone else, to keep a modicum of happiness. And, anyway, I'm a doctor sometimes but right now I'm trying to get the best price for my silver Peugeot that's just failed an MOT.

I look around me. Cars are piled up like rotting metallic carcasses. The May sun turns the rusted bumpers into colours that remind me of rose leaves just as they come out.

"Do you think you could help me Doc?" Paul says.

I nod but I don't say anything.

"It's the insurance, my life insurance; I just need the form signed. Can you just sign it here?"

He runs words together as he speaks, Paul does. Great long words without gaps, like the way they do German words. Canyoujustsignit. That's one word.

"Just send it up to the health centre, I can do it there," I say.

I take on this sort of barrier, an iron curtain to protect myself. It's just like killdeer. I'm hiding myself behind my profession, or behind something else, or perhaps it's disguise, or whatever, I'm not really sure. Sometimes life can get complicated.

"That'll take bloody ages!" Paul says.

Although Paul is crooked, I'm certain that his face is physically crooked too. In addition he has that menacing smile, which he unfurls at this moment. It is not a smile of happiness.

I am scared of people like Paul. I am, in addition, very keen to be liked. It's a weak intangible situation that anyone can abuse. Paul, because he sort of specialises in that fast quick assessment, knows both these facts.

As it happens, I've just looked through Paul's record. That was after the first time I met him. He came in because he was a new patient and I always see the new patients. I remember him partly because, well, a man like Paul you sort of remember. He is a breath from another place.

He has no medical records to speak of. He has never been ill, just a few earaches as a child. It's strange that all of us have this storybook, sitting dustily on a surgery shelf; a whole book of our lives, all the way back to the yellow and brown archives of our youth.

It's just that Paul hasn't got any pages in his.

I'm saying all this because I'm trying to find mitigation for what happens later. There is a strong feeling that I sometimes succumb to, especially during a morning of work, but in reality almost anywhere, that we are really just pathways that cross, and these crossing, when we meet someone, the threads come temporarily together so that the maps of our lives are laid, like trails on the fabric of the world, forming a fine irregular lattice work. Rather like a leaf that has composted down to its skeleton or as an ornately carved Iranian window might do with the light. And, if we extend this further, these meetings should then be marked with cairns so that, should we become lost, we can retrace our mental steps and find out where we have gone wrong.

I often return to this particular cairn. It's got plenty of stones on it. But whatever I wished I had done, I sign his form for him and he touches my arm and smiles at me. It's a sincere smile this time; he is really pleased. I see for the first time a hidden side to Paul, something rough and well disguised but beautiful in itself.

I remember Paul particularly because he is the new partner of Maria. Maria, I have known for years. Now she *really* has a story wrapped up inside those medical records sitting there on the shelf. A story that few people can possibly imagine. They speak of people like that mountaineer who broke his leg in the Andes and managed to survive, they call people like him a survivor, when actually it's Maria who is the survivor; he hasn't been through anything like what Maria has endured.

Maria is an exceptional person. In fact, if this story has any theme to it, I would say it could be called the many exceptional things about Maria. However, this might come across a bit "Sound of Music" which I assure you it absolutely isn't. Maria is just about the most complicated screwed up person I have ever met. The extent of this will not become clear until the end. There is a secret language in the medical world, a code not fit for public knowledge, this would describe Maria as a "Heartsink" patient. You see her name on the list and inwardly you feel, oh no, not her. Except its peculiar because, although my heart should sink, for she has almost every diagnosis, both mental and physical, known to man, attended with a very manipulative personality, in fact I enjoy seeing her, she fascinates me.

So when Paul finally comes to see me, the first time I meet him, I already know plenty about him. Maria has told me. She hadn't had much joy with men, which is putting it mildly.

"Paul is different to all the others," she says. "I think he really likes me."

Then there is a long pause and Maria looks down and her eyes nearly shut. She takes a deep breath. She often talks like this: great long pauses, deep breaths, eyes closed as she tries to say things. I would have thought it was for dramatic effect, but I think it's just the ridiculous number of tablets she takes.

At the end of the pause she says, "I don't know, I can't tell what it is. He is a good person. He just likes me."

For me, the best part about Paul is that I've never seen Maria so happy. She's had her times, Maria, but that day, when they come in together, she shines; there is that light in her eyes that I've not really seen before, like the filmic layer of tears over her eyes has changed entirely in its consistency, and her eyes themselves have become darker and clearer. There must be a better way of explaining these clichés that surround love.

Paul is from Bristol but a month ago he managed to get hold of the council flat above Maria. He only has a two month contract but they told him that's standard these days, so that they can rid themselves of nuisance tenants. It means that the whole house is theirs. Some things make me feel happy and this is one of them. I like it too when Chelsea lose and when England win. I like May as well; makes me feel like I could sing inside.

I like Paul for what he's done for Maria. Life can be so simple if you let it. Is that why I just sign his form for him. It just all seems so simple to me at this point. I find, though, that when life is feeling simple, you're just not seeing it right, you're not watching carefully enough. Life is never simple; there is intrigue and drama everywhere you look. There is no children's book or Julie Andrews to life. It's complex and periodically very painful. And that's the worst bit; the pain doesn't get shared around very evenly so that people like Maria get huge quantities and I suppose people like me get off lightly. Or, anyway, it can seem like that.

The car wrecker's is down near the Bristol road. When I drive down this road, it always feels as though I'm coming off the end of the Cotswolds. Down Limcombe Hill, surfing on a gigantic wave, and out in front of you is the broad flat flood plain of the river Severn with The Wetlands and Ardley Castle out in the distance. It's one of those areas that has a sudden dramatic change in its geography: the end of England. The climate itself feels different.

The man at the wrecker's comes out to Paul and me as we are talking. He wears a red overall. Alan, his name is. I know everyone around here and even worse everyone knows me. Walking down the street in Wormbridge, I know how it feels to be Posh and Becks, except no one wants to take my photo, I'm not a size nought and I'm pretty rubbish at football. Alan is a calm man who used to work at Bristol Airport. But after 6 months it became too much for him; he had a breakdown and moved back to Ardley village. He is a simple, wise man, who is always kind and says things that reverberate in your head for days afterwards, although at the time they don't seem very important. He looks my car up and down. He took this place on because some uncle of his who ran it got sick and died, just as Alan was recovering from his breakdown. Now it suits him down to the ground, as the cliché goes. It's as though the place has absorbed some of his simple wisdom and he has become, in himself, partly a breaker's yard.

Paul is standing next to him as he sizes up my car. He asks me what it failed on. I tell him mainly the brakes, the differential and all 4 tyres.

He and Paul look it up and down. Alan looks under the bonnet. I notice the silver birch again. I'm always noticing irrelevant things, as though I'm not concentrating. There is a split up the side of the still young trunk. But the mottled shade it gives is beautiful like a Scandinavian spring.

The Peugeot I'm trying to rid myself of is also silver. There is nothing beautiful about this however.

Alan decides, in the end, he will take it off my hands but that it's not worth anything.

"Just don't get money for wrecks any more," he says, "not since they changed the landfill laws, too expensive to get rid of them. Look how many I've got." He points vaguely to his large yard.

Walking around there it's like being a survivor after Armageddon, or an archaeologist or something. Each vehicle, stacked one on top of another, has a story to divulge as well: of the day perhaps it was brought, the first proud owner, moments of affection, arguments, all those things that go on in cars. Except now the cars are dead, gone, like a cemetery of sorts.

"No money in it now, apart from spares," Alan is saying. Then he goes all quiet and thoughtful. It's as though there are different voices or writers in his head and he is listening to them, except that isn't the case because I asked him once.

"That differential," he starts again, Paul is barely listening. "I think about that differential joint sometimes. They say it was the only part of a motorcar - when they made the first ones, back hundred years ago - it was the only part that wasn't already invented. All the rest was there, just waiting to be put together: the internal combustion engine, the drive shaft, the wheel brakes. They had all those things before, it was just the differential joint they were waiting for so the bloody thing could go around corners."

I nod but I'm not really listening. It is days afterwards that I think about it again.

He takes it in the end, the whole car, minus the radio, which I rip out. The cassette player is bust but the radio is still good.

Alan takes the keys and then scratches the back of his head. He always does that, one hand on his fattening belly the other at the back of his head scratching. I don't think his scalp is actually itchy, it's simply a mannerism.

Then Paul says, "How you going to get back to Wormbridge?"

He smiles at me again but it's gone back to being a crooked leer, since I signed that form.

"I was going to hitch," I say.

It's only 3 miles back into town, up the hill, back into the Cotswolds, back into England. But I feel sort of at his mercy and he feels like I'm sort of at his mercy and he seems to like that. I was brought up to be wary of accepting help, as you may have to pay it back. Getting in debt. My dad never got in debt. He was almost obsessional about that. Never get in anyone's debt, it leaves you weaker, but I try to never follow my dad's advice.

So I take a lift in the Mercedes.

Paul's skin, I notice, is brown. He's got a watch mark on his left wrist. It makes him swarthy, even more like a man you shouldn't trust. But then this is just a cultural thing. Me, I'm from middle class, middle income, middle ability, mittel Europe. He's from somewhere deeper down in England and sometimes it's like a culture shock. I feel unprepared, a little lost, slightly shocked in fact.

We get to talking. He asks me if I hitchhike a lot and I tell him I used to but now I drive everywhere, it's all part of the money/time ratio that stays constant throughout our lives.

"How d'you mean?" he says.

I say that if you add the amount of money you earn to the amount of spare time you have, you always get the same number. He likes that, he laughs out loud and feels his shaven head with the palm of his hand.

He tells me that I'm right there, and that he personally prefers to have more of the money and less of the time.

"I've got loads of that time business to spare," he says.

It's the other way round for me: I'm looking up the other end of the ratio to him, but I decide not to say that.

"If I could just swap some time for some money, that would be nice," says Paul and we smile at each other.

"So, do you do a lot of mechanic stuff yourself?" I ask him.

"What, fiddling with nasty oily motors. No. hate it. Someone just dented my door. And they drove off, the fucker."

I nod as a way of agreeing with him. Then there is a long, slightly awkward pause.

"So where did you get that tan?" I ask him.

Hitchhiking is probably the best training for being a doctor. You just have to talk to someone no matter whether you've got anything in common. I was shy as a boy and hitching forced me to talk. I was swapping talk for miles. It's easy and sort of brainless. Now I can talk to anyone. My precious little upbringing left me cosseted and inadequate. That's the trouble being an only child. It just doesn't teach you the more important lessons, like how to share, and how to talk to someone else. But I'm better now. I can get talking to just about anyone.

"Just got back from Mexico," Paul says.

"Mexico, whereabouts?" I ask him. I'm expecting him to say Cancun, because, well, it looks like a sort of Cancun tan.

He is oddly evasive. "Down south," he says.

"The Yucatan" I say.

"What?" he says. It is clear he hasn't heard of the Yucatan.

"Whereabouts did you go?" I repeat. He looks a bit confused, uncomfortable, like he is a kid and has just lied, that sort of face. I notice he has a small silver stud earring in his left ear and he is chewing something.

"Place called St Cristobel."

"I've been there," I tell him and I try and talk about the village a few kilometres away, where, in one of the churches, they worship a coca cola bottle.

"Yeah, I heard about it." Paul says, except his heart is not in this conversation. "One of the Brothers lived near there," he continued. "They say they shot a westerner who tried to take a photo of that coca cola bottle. Killed him."

"Yeah, I heard about that as well. Strange feeling up there." And I carry on in my banal way and I don't really think he's listening, since he keeps fiddling with his ear stud.

"Wheredoyou live then?" Paul asks, when I finally stop. It comes out as one word, nearly.

"Herdsley." I say.

It sort of defines me, living there, not in Wormbridge. It's just slightly more expensive and everyone in Wormbridge wrinkles their nose and purses their top lip when I say I live there. It makes me feel like lying, but I used to lie a lot about things like this and I've made a pact with myself that I'm not going to do it any more. So I don't and sure enough he wrinkles his nose.

In Wormbridge, he lets me out next to the old post office, with it's immaculate red brick and odd machines glimpsed through frosted windows. It's sort of fascist in there, I always think, for no good or rational reason. He isn't going any further and I can walk the rest of the way.

"Yeah, thanks," I say.

"Thanks for signing me up, Doc."

I cringe inside and smile at him. I notice the corners of his mouth are defined and curve in a lovely way.

I close the door and walk past the ironmongers advertising reduced price key cutting and some dodgy looking paint that's being sold half price.

That was the second time I met Paul.

The third time was up in his room. By then, though, he was dead.

# CHAPTER TWO

They say that Eminem has a tattoo on his left wrist. Or maybe it's his right, I don't quite remember. It says, apparently, cut here.

I always think that the problem for Maria is that she hasn't got such explicit instructions. Perhaps, if she had, it would be easier.

Maria is a complex and very difficult patient. She self harms to such an alarming degree it's a shock, really, that she's still alive. She will overdose on anything she can get her hands on. If there are no tablets available she will cut herself. When the knives are taken away she resorts to scrubbing her face with a toothbrush. She's even been known to just repeatedly slap herself, or just scratch herself viciously. She is continually in and out of Fairmead, the psychiatric institution, that locally, has become a byword for the insane. As in, she should be in Fairmead, which is usually true. I suppose I want to tell you about Maria so that you can see why I have acted as I do.

One thing I have learnt as a doctor is that there is plenty of very strange things going on in peoples lives. Mostly, though, people hide them.

Maria is different because she doesn't hide them, instead she wears them on, or in reality under, her sleeve.

In truth though, she is playing a game. She is playing killdeer. It's a dangerous game and the stakes, as it turns out, are pretty high.

She abuses drugs. She used to take illegal ones but now exclusively she takes ones that I supply her with. I am her pusher, it might be said except truly I am trying to help her. She takes all kinds of rubbish: painkillers, anti depressants, anti-inflammatories, sedatives, anti psychotics, odd little pills for dizziness, basically anything she can get her hands on. Sometimes she sees other doctors and gets all sorts of other crap as well.

She has a son, Bernard, who is a poor mute boy who desperately tries to somehow keep ahead of her. Bernard can't speak because of something that happened at birth. Too many drugs, not enough air, something like that. Poor Bernard, everyone says, not being able to speak and having Maria as a mother. He hides everything he can. Sometimes she finds a knife, her favourite is a Stanley Knife, and since she has no specific instruction, like Eminem has, she cuts anywhere. She hides blades where she thinks he won't find them. She's got some favourite spots. He can never quite keep up with her butchery so that every time she cuts, he feels he has failed in some way. When the knives and blades are all gone, she uses her nails. He actually cuts her nails for her.

Often he comes in to see me without her and pleads with me for pills. He pleads like a beggar. It's an odd performance: no discernable words but this high-pitched whine. I know plenty of addicts and he has the same desperate bit between his teeth. The only difference is that he is an addict by proxy only. He is procuring for someone else. He knows what will happen without the pills. It's one of those stupid conversations where, first of all, he is writing everything down, so it's very slow. Second of all we are both speaking in a sort of code, a parallel conversation.

The pills are for his mother. I know. He knows. Life can be a charade like that, all of us pretending something and lying and deceiving. It's just that if he says that the pills are for Maria then I can't give them to him. We've got strict limits on that. So if he doesn't say they are for Maria, then I might give him some, even though I know they are for his Mother. Anything can get complicated if you let it.

I've never liked charades. Charades and killdeer are very closely related. I play neither particularly well. But I play my part because, I suppose, it's easier: easy for me, easy for Bernard, easy for Maria. Easier for the whole damn world. It doesn't mean I feel any happier about doing it.

Sometimes they admit Maria to the psychiatric ward, when the cutting really does become too much. They try to make her tackle her past and she cuts herself so badly it barely seems worth it.

When Maria is back living at home she comes in

to see me. This is before she has met Paul. She walks like a cripple although there is nothing wrong with her legs. The new drugs they have her on from The Royal have kind of taken away her fight: she is flaccid, paralysed, drifting but without any real reason to get anywhere. And she's still cutting away, in a strange sort of triumph.

Maria plays a lot of killdeer. Now, killdeer can be played by anyone. Often everyone is playing it together. I read about it from Tom Spanbauer in his novel The Man Who Fell in Love with the Moon. It's a book we must all read. Since I've read it, his notion has informed what I do as a doctor. It's my golden rule. Put simply, it describes how a bird, called a killdeer, behaves when it is being hunted. How it fakes an injury and leads the predator away from what is most precious, most important. In the birds case it usually her young. So in psychological terms, killdeer is when a person pretends there is something wrong with them to lead you away from a problem that is far more serious, or important. It is essentially a manipulation, a lie, for it needs the person to feign illness and draw attention to this, so that we never find what is really happening. And, although it's a conscious manipulation, it is done to deliberately mislead, it can, if repeated often enough, become real in itself, this illness.

It makes all of us actors, in a way, which we are of course, although we act with our lives and we are impelled, we have no choice. We can't ever come out of role for if we do, we will give away our true sickness, our weakness which we at all times protect and hide. Once we understand this, as doctors, we can then avoid or ignore what is happening in front of us and instead look at what is giving rise to this deception. For there is little point in finding a cure because the patient has no wish to be relieved of their symptom. After all there is no way to make someone better who doesn't want to be. It's hopeless and pointless, and if you did, by luck or drugs, cure one of the problems, then another would simply sprout in its place, like an awful medusa in a nightmare animation.

So, when it comes to Maria, this is why she is on so many medicines. Doctors have vainly been trying to cure what are her killdeer symptoms, but she doesn't want to stop cutting because this, somehow and very obscurely, keeps us from delving where she really doesn't want us delving.

We all play killdeer, to some extent. Maria is an expert, as I am about to find out. And it works because the cutting is so awful, none of us ever get round to finding out why she is so screwed up. So now she is sitting in front of me and says she needs to tell me something. Whether this is genuine or not, I don't know.

I say, "Maria, what did you want to say?"

She responds to her name and manages to raise her eyes to my level, but only for a moment, as though some heavy weight is tied to them that doesn't allow them to look at me any longer than a few moments.

She mumbles something and I draw a little nearer. This is going to take some time. Everything with Maria takes some time. I'm already late and now she has decided that this is the day she will tell me something. I'm late but I would not miss this for the world.

I stay silent. Perhaps I am learning from Bernard. Perhaps this is the only way to be with Maria.

There's a really deep and deathly silence and if it's a game we're playing it's who can withstand the silence for longest, like not licking your lips when you are eating doughnuts. Finally she starts talking.

"It's before…what happened before…."

Then she stops. I don't know how to get her going again. She is stubborn like her son and this must be the hundredth time I've seen her and I still am not sure how to get her going. So I wait.

Finally she says, "I need to talk to someone."

It's as though she started up at killdeer again. The only way to get round a decent game of killdeer is to be blunt and honest. So I ask her straight out.

"Did something bad happen to you?"

She nods.

"Who was it Maria?" There, that was the second naming.

She starts speaking. And then, like a guilty cloud is coming over her, she goes quiet again.

"What happened Maria?" I must stop saying her name.

She winces a little and her eyes close entirely. "The Brothers…" she says.

"What, your brothers did something to you?" I say.

I, for my part, am playing a different game, a sort of reverse cerebral killdeer, where I am trying to guess what it is she is hiding, what she is leading me away from.

"Did they hurt you?" I say.

She nods her head.

Whether it's something I said or what, but that's it from Maria. She closes up completely and I realize that I haven't learnt enough from Bernard. I need to shut up a little more. She is trying to show me something, trying to lead me somewhere and I cock it up. Then she stands up and sits down and we talk about the drugs from the hospital after her latest admission. I realize that Maria is getting to a stage where she wants to get all this off her chest: she wants to talk. She says she was trying to find someone to tell in hospital and no one would listen. Not how she wanted anyhow.

"The cuts," I say, and she pulls back her sleeves.

Her arms give me a shock. Eminem might have a neat little cut on the right or the left wrist, but Maria's arms are more like a ploughed field or the sky after an air show. Most of her arm is just scar tissue now. Healed and pale and ghastly, like a piece of pork made ready for the oven.

I often wonder what it's like being Maria: what thoughts, what logic goes on within her. I can't see where this cutting business is going or where it's from or for that matter what it's for. There are other ways of playing killdeer that the rest of us find acceptable. What is it about Maria?

I asked her once, maybe two years ago, about the cutting. She said it let the pain out, as though pain was like blood that could be released. I said she had to find another way to get rid of the pain, so then she asked me for more painkillers to which I answered no. So we didn't get very far.

So I still really wonder what it's like to be Maria. She comes to the verge of leading me to where the truth lies, but now she's made a sudden decision not to go there. Will it help if we do ever get there? What can I do apart from listen and be empathetic? I am not a commando or some magician, or even a detective.

I ask her whether she'll come back in a week's time. She says yes. I say we'll talk again, then and she nods and for a moment she raises her eyes.

Sometimes I think people who come and see me are sort of testing me out first. Making sure I'm worthy of their treasure. Maria is doing something like that. Or at least that's what I think she's doing.

So I allow her to leave the room with her secrets and her demons all intact. I have no idea what the family has done to this woman: the father, the brothers. I have an inkling but maybe that's just my imagination.

I know a lot about Maria. Well, at least I think I do. She used to be a junkie. Because of all her pills, she has the complexion of Heroin, but she's been clean for three years. It wasn't that she particularly wanted to stop, it was just that the supply ran out and she managed to get some benzos from her doctor, not me I hasten to add, and she told me she just locked herself in and took huge quantities of pills and sweated it out.

A proper British Heroine. Anyway, she told me she preferred the benzos: diazepam or temazepam, it made little difference. They did to her what she needed: unravelled her insides, stopped the ever more voracious and circular thoughts that whirred around in her and tightened her up. Then she got addicted to them. That's sort of stabilized now, although she still has them. Bernard hands them out each morning and he hides the rest. One of the best places, he told me once, was underneath the push chair in the front garden but then she found them, inadvertently, when she was lying out on the unmown grass. And took them all at once.

I get plenty of detail on her life, but she has never talked about her family, or her brothers or anything that is really important like what has happened to this woman to make her cut herself so insatiably.

When she comes back a week later she's met Paul and all she wants to talk about is Paul and how she met him and how he's different to the others etc etc. So I missed my opportunity right there at the start. I could have cut a whole lot of corners if I had known. If I had kept my trap shut. But I'm learning. All I can really ask is that I learn from my mistakes.

It sounds so simple.

## CHAPTER THREE

One thing happens at this point.

The cutting stops. All Maria can talk about is Paul, when I next see her. Paul, Paul.

Within a week her life has turned around and she looks fantastic, her hair is clean, she seems taller and has beautiful clean green eyes. The cutting has stopped and she doesn't want to talk about it. I realise how weak drugs are compared to life and how this medical profession is just scratching away at the periphery of things.

As a couple, Maria and Paul are a strange combination. People stare at Maria. Her eyes are pale green, almost grey. She moves in a way that is simple and elegant, like a dancer or an actress. Her nose is thin with slightly revealed nostrils and it's flattened below the tip as though someone has sanded it down gently. Her mouth is full and she has a way of revealing her teeth that make her lips almost touchable.

Paul is the opposite extreme. It's as though someone has been asked to draw an ugly, crooked looking man. He is a caricature. It later becomes clear that he is an entirely good person; his looks, however, are incompatible with this.

She is set up now. The contract on her council flat lasts for 6 months and they say it's just a formality to renew it. Upstairs, before Paul moves in, there's a very tired looking man who is on the gear and hardly ever appears apart from to stagger down to the shops and round the back to Eddies to pick up some more ten pound bags and disappear back up the steps. His contract is up in a month but he doesn't look as though he's going to make it that far even.

And sure enough he dies, just about when his contract is up. I know because I have to certify him dead in his room. Heroin overdose, the post mortem says. The gear was different to what he was used to. How pathetic he looked up there, lying on the bed, unwanted by anyone. So now it's all perfectly set up so Paul can move in.

Maria told me once how she loved swallowing pills. She loves how they rattle in her mouth before they go down. She can swallow hundreds at a time; she is well practiced. Sometimes she thinks she should be a drug mule. She told me that once. I told her that she should get *Maria Full of Grace* out on dvd, that would put her off. She laughed because it was about a girl called Maria, who, by circumstances, becomes a cocaine mule and swallows loads of condoms stuffed full of coke.

Later she came to see me all angry.

"You didn't tell me it was some fucking foreign language and we had to read the writing!"

I told her I didn't want her swearing when in the surgery and she waves me away, her eyes are still angry but at least they are open.

I asked her, did she finish the film, and she said yeah. She was sullen, like I had ripped her off in some way.

"So do you still fancy being a mule?" I asked her.

She shook her head. But I hadn't won. She made me realise I hadn't won, because *the film was in some fucking foreign language.*

All she wants to speak about now is how she had first met Paul. She tells me everything does Maria, well nearly everything, in the end.

She first met Paul with some rather unsavoury characters from her past. It was at her uncle Stanley's birthday party. She hates her family. She never made much of a secret of that. Her father, she didn't know, her mother is self-serving and cares nothing for Maria or her brother. She liked her older brother, he was wild but he was always kind to her. Except he had too big a habit to support so that not even a daily burglary was enough. His stealing was like a cow eating grass, he just had to do it all the time, almost without thinking. Inevitably he got caught so now he was in prison. Uncle Stanley, her mother's brother, had done some things before for which she was grateful. She wanted to see him and it was being said that he didn't have long to live.

So she's at this party, dolled up like she always used to be, with a few monsters from her past. The current stepfather is fawning all over her mother, who is pissed and her massive cleavage is in danger of falling out of the tight blouse she's wearing. The party's in a reception room upstairs at the Prince of Wales pub.

Almost everyone has a lit fag to their lips. Maria is talking to a friend of her first stepfather, not the current one. There has been a few. This friend is called Clive. She knew him before and she didn't want to carry on knowing him. He has inexplicably made it rich and is trying to sell his old Mercedes, since he has just lined up in the car park below a brand new 7 series BMW with all the trimmings. She has never liked him. She never liked her first stepfather, either. He had left on Maria's eighth birthday. Afterwards they said there were irregularities. You can't just go and cross the brothers. Mum had said that he wasn't coming back and there, in Maria, were the first feelings of happiness that she could remember. That he was gone for good.

So this man is trying to sell her an old Mercedes and wants her to come and have a burn in his new BMW 7 series, and probably a quick fondle as well, when Paul walks up.

There is not much heroic about Paul. He is short, quite narrow shouldered, ugly apart from the corners of his mouth, which are curved in an unusual way. Clive, the ex friend of the first stepfather, is fat, flabby but smooth and has something cruel running around his face.

So Paul comes walking up to them, just as Maria is fearful that this Clive is about to force her to come for a drive. It feels heroic, him coming up then, something like a movie, Maria tells me. He comes up and says that he wants to buy a Mercedes and he couldn't help hearing that there was one up for grabs. Then he smiles sideways at Maria, like he knows something. He's got a crooked and toothy smile, like he doesn't really care what you think of him.

They talk Mercedes for a while, as the room fills - like a snowstorm paperweight - with smoke. This room is long and thin with windows on both sides, like a ship of sorts. Sun comes through the window and its path to the floor is sharply delineated by all the smoke in a series of slanting silver columns.

Maria manages to slip away as the men do their car talk. She sits next to the wheezing uncle, the birthday boy who once got her out of trouble and took her away.

He has lung cancer, Mother had told her, and there wasn't much longer for him, which was lucky, he is joking, because the lease on their pub was running out in about three weeks time, and he might not be able to renegotiate.

He, with Aunty Midge, ran the Prince of Wales and allowed everyone to smoke upstairs.

They swapped excuses for not giving up, Maria said she was having a hard time of it, Stanley said he had terminal cancer, the best excuse there was. Uncle was laughing at his own joke and squeezed Maria's hand that lay in her lap. "Incurable cancer!" he repeated, and laughed again.

Maria said she can't believe they can't do something but Uncle Stanley just shakes his head. He's always been a bit different from the rest of the family. Although he's a piss-head and on the make if anything dodgy is around, he does have a sort of respect for everyone, in so much that he doesn't steal off anyone, apart from corporations. That's his rule, no stealing.

"Surprised that fat man with the new car has the nerve to talk to you Maria," he says. They are looking over at Paul talking to Clive. "Mind you he sort of helped you out in the end, didn't he, by dobbing that scumbag husband of my sister's to the mercy of the Brothers. Got one big weirdo off the scene didn't he. Not sure how he's made it so big. I think he found God himself, or something like that. Just lucky for him he didn't become a Brother, he's always just done their dirty work. Perhaps he has got more sense than it appears from his fat self satisfied face."

Then he laughs again, but this time the laugh turns in to a cough and the cough becomes intractable and Maria is rubbing his back hopelessly. Stanley and Midge are just about the only people in the family, apart from her brother, who look out for Maria. She hates the way he's named after a knife that she keeps in store for the worst days. Uncle Stanley looked after her once and she won't ever forget it. She was in a very vulnerable condition, she knew more than she should and it was the first time the Brothers had got paranoid. The whole world seemed to be riven with paranoia around her family. The stepfather was the first to go and slowly, one by one, Brothers were disappearing. So Stanley and Midge had hid her until everything calmed down, in their own way they tried to limit the damage. So she tries to hang around as Stanley coughs his guts out, so that he can protect her again.

But Midge steers him out of the way and out of the room, until the coughing has dried up, so Maria's left on her own again.

Before she knows what is happening, Paul has her by the arm and they are in Clive's car, going down to his house. She's been this way before and it wasn't very nice and some fear starts building up in her so that she feels like cutting. She digs her nails into her hands and then looks over at Paul, sitting on the other side of the back seat, and its odd but all the fear goes. She isn't frightened.

I'm already half an hour late in the surgery, but Maria has never talked so openly, and I'm not going to mess up this time. See how I'm learning.

So they stand round the Mercedes, out the back of his newly built, palatial, mock Cotswold stone villa. He used to be a builder but this is too rich for a builder now. He has business interests instead.

The Mercedes is a pale yellow, almost brown coloured and sits like an old man; grand, gracious and very much out of fashion, next to the new sleek mucular, testosterone of the BMW.

"Classic car," Clive says, after a period. "It's an absolute steal for £2,000. In a couple of years these 230's will be worth ten grand at least. Mark my words."

Paul nods. Maria looks away. Every word this man says makes her wince, inwardly, like a contraction.

Men get funny with cars and start talking all loud and know it all. They tap things and look perplexed, they look behind seats and deep into a machine whose only secrets you might need to know are well hidden.

"Two grand is what I want for it and I'm not a bargaining man."

The way he looks he doesn't look like a bargaining man. He's overweight and pleased with himself. He reeks of new money.

"I've known you, what, four years, Paul? You never had two ten pence pieces to rub together. How can you afford this?"

Paul grins all crookedly. Maria notices he is smaller than her and that his head looks too big for the rest of his body. He's all wrong but there's something about him.

He answers that there's been a bit of business. Maria doesn't know what business actually means but there seems to be a lot of it around here.

"Two grand is it? Well I need a car." Paul talks sometimes like he's talking to himself.

Behind them there is what looks like a quadruple garage with two doors, both of which are controlled by a button somewhere on his keys.

"I'd like to take it out, y'know before I hand over the readies."

Clive looks excited at this, as though his plan has somehow come off.

Maria is stiffening up.

He throws the keys to Paul, and then he says to Maria, "I'll mix you up a nice Bloody Mary, while we're waiting."

Paul looks from one to the other, as he lets keys from the ring slip down his fingers. He's thinking but he resignedly gets in the car and slowly winds down the window.

"Press that button for the gates at the front."

He starts up the car. Already Maria is being shown into the house through the front door.

The big ostentatious gates open up, like some sewage floodgates. Then the engine dies.

Paul shouts out, "Hey Maria, aint you coming?"

There is a pause, and some strange sound reverberates in her head.

"I want to know if you like it."

"Yeah I'll come," Maria says.

The fat Clive, ex-friend of her ex-stepfather smiles like the grand dame that he is. But it's a hollow smile.

They drive off and they don't say anything. The gate closes behind them. The car glides like all posh cars glide.

"So what d'ya think?' Paul says. He talks fast and short does Paul.

"He's a twat, that's what I think!"

"About the car, stupid." Paul's big head turns round to her and he shows his teeth; they're big and crooked.

Maria thinks for a bit and then says, "The car, I like the car."

They drive down towards Wormbridge. He drives slow and languid; the car sweeps in its movements, down past Hardwick, Ardley through the dog ends of Limcombe.

There is mostly silence between them. Maria feels nervous, on edge. She is not used to being out of the world she knows. But she feels less nervous than ten minutes ago. That is something.

"Shall we try the radio?" Maria says.

Paul says he hates the radio and all the crap music. He's dour and then he smiles again.

The country around them is changing to hills and smaller lanes. Summer is very nearly here but it's been raining and there's a sour smell to the earth as well.

"Where you going?" Maria asks him. She's suspicious. "Can't you just take me home?" she says a little while later.

Paul says, "I wanted to take you somewhere nice, show you a good view."

"What and have a quick fondle and maybe a fuck if it's on offer?!"

Maria darts back at him.

He stops the car in a shallow lay by. Turns off the engine.

"Look Maria, I promise not too touch you at all. You have my word. Come on, let's walk up this hill, you'll like it. I won't even come near you."

He gets out of the car. She sits sullenly in the passenger seat.

"The frigging frying pan to the fucking fire!' she says.

"Look Maria, I don't even want to fuck you. It's just a good view. Come on."

It's like dogs and children and killdeer. You just have to walk away and they always follow. Well mostly anyway. You just have to have the nerve to do it.

So Paul walks to the five bar gate and starts

climbing over it. Over on the other side he hears a click as the car door shuts. He doesn't look around. He knows about frightened animals. When he was a boy he worked at weekends down the RSPCA kennels on the top of the hill above Herdsley. Keep your distance, act like you don't really care and above all show no fear.

"Ain't you helping?" she shouts out. Then she mutters, "No manners, no idea how to treat a woman."

"I ain't supposed to touch you Maria. So I'm not."

She climbs over the gate.

I know the walk up Smallpox Hill. Paul is right, the view is great up there. You have a feeling that you're on an island and the sea was here once but now it's gone and you're sitting high and dry and nothing else really matters. You see all the small cars and their little lives and Wormbridge at the end of the valley, hunkered down against the weather and you feel above all of that, all high and dry, beyond it all.

She tells me how she struggles up that hill and he's as good as his word, he walks about 10 yards in front and checks occasionally to make sure she's okay. She struggles and she's short of breath. She curses the smoking. By the top, she feels quite dizzy, so she lies down and looks up at the strange avenue of trees up above her. When she sits up she looks out over the other way, over Limcombe Hill and down towards the Severn, the end of England, and the Welsh hills stretching right back to Skirrid and the Black Mountains. He is sitting about 6 yards away. It's all getting a bit stupid so Maria gets up and sits down next to him.

She tries to show him where her house is. She's never before realized why Queen's Hill is called a hill, except now she can see it, although she can't make out her house. She can see where Wormbridge peters out just as the Cotswolds peters out down Limcombe and Style Hill.

There are remains on the top, of where the smallpox victims used to live, isolated, segregated by the world. There are big craters in the ground, and a strange atmosphere, an atmosphere full of something unnameable. It's not fear and its not glory. I sometimes think this hill does stuff, something spiritual, some arch effect so that people act differently, as though a spirit overcomes you. I tell Maria that. Maria doesn't agree.

So they walk back down again. They don't say anything.

Back at the car he begins swearing wildly. Someone has left a long gash down the driver side door, it's caved in a little.

"Oh fuck, I'll have to buy it now," Paul says.

"I like it anyway, I'm glad you're going to buy it." Maria doesn't smile but she looks up at him. That's something.

He takes her back to Queen's Hill.

"I'm sorry about your Uncle by the way."

Maria just shrugs. She's about to get out of the car. "Thanks for bringing me home."

They sit in silence for a while. It feels like an age because Maria is thinking desperately what to say next.

Perhaps, without thinking, she should lean over and kiss him on the lips. It's such a long way, though, in a Mercedes that her legs would be left dangling in midair. So she doesn't. She doesn't know what to do next, so she sits back in the passenger seat.

"What are you going to do about the door?"

"Oh I'll be alright, I'll get another from the breakers yard. Shame though. They never look quite the same."

She makes a sympathetic noise. She isn't really used to making the running. In the end she gets out and does a sort of silly wave at him and then immediately regrets it.

The pram in the front garden nearly trips her, but he is gone by then. So she looks under it, careful and thorough, to see whether there are a few of those pill pots.

There aren't any.

# CHAPTER FOUR

I sometimes think, how the hell did I end up in Wormbridge. We all are complicated, we think we know exactly what we're doing. We have come to our position in life through a meandering set of decisions and choices, and it is easy enough to end up somewhere that you never intended. It's also easy enough to say what the hell am I doing here, and it doesn't really help.

There is Rosie. I need to tell you about Rosie because we have been going for three years. It's not like we're attached. We're separate and then sometimes we are together. I suppose that I love her. It might sound cold and heartless but quite honestly I don't know. She has a luscious, peony like character: rich like dark red. Maybe that's why I love her, or perhaps I love her because I find her this attractive, or maybe she is this attractive because I love her.

It's difficult to be sure sometimes, what leads to

what and when to whom.

Rosie is a gardener. Now I've known a few gardeners and, broadly, they can be split into two types. The fighters, the ones that find nature continually a challenge, an object that has to be beaten, conquered, subdued. And then there are nurturers. The nurturers are different. People, like Rosie, who help nature and are therefore helped by nature as well. The fighters' gardens often look tidier and well tended but the real beauty of the natural world is absent. The scruffier, nurturers' gardens are less controlled, nature has been allowed to show itself off; resplendent like a Quetzal or a Peacock. Maybe in life, people can also be divided like this. I've never really thought about it.

Rosie's gardens often have what others would call weeds propagating themselves: magnificent, like nomadic kings. Flowering geraniums, poppies blown in from the big fields of corn down in the Severn valley, Oregerons that thrust themselves out of the cracks between the paving slabs, the flowers like sirens on the sides of lighthouses.

Weeds, she will say, are simply flowers that are not where they're meant to be. Weeds are a man-made invention; they do not exist in nature.

Rosie is dark haired, she has recently used henna so that now her hair is full and shines like a blackcurrant bush. Her face is slightly freckled. But you don't need to know all this detail. I am getting carried away.

Rosie is just about my whole life, not counting Mother and a few friends who drink too much and do too little. She lives in a tiny village a few miles from Herdsley, where all the old actors and artists retire to. Just recently I've spent more time at Rosie's house than my own rather dour little cottage on a steep hill above Herdsley valley and below Smallpox Hill. Rosie's house has something that mine doesn't have and I'm not sure what exactly it is. Something like women and Frida Kahlo and flowers and a heart and soul.

Otherwise I have a contract to supply medical services to the people of Wormbridge. I am their doctor, for better or worse. Strange things happen as a doctor, sometimes, but the majority of the time it's morning surgery, visits to ill people who cannot get to the surgery, the evening surgery, then home.

Life is that litany.

So, for the last few years I've been chuntering along like this, week in, week out, following this rather dull melody and staying sufficiently separate and uninvolved. Then, quite out of the blue, two things happen that sort of unsettle me, fracture that litany.

I remember the police ringing me that day. It is in the afternoon and I thought I'd done all my visits. One of our patients has been found in the back streets of Wormbridge, dead in his flat. Although death is one of the more constant things in life compared to, say, disease and illness, for some reason I am needed. I am the death sayer: no one is dead, technically, until I say they are. At times I feel like: why do I have to say? Its pretty damn obvious when someone becomes a stiff, has lost his twenty-one grams, has ceased to be.

I remember it particularly because of what happens later but also because the day before had been even stranger. I am having a bad run. Normally death is death, but I am beginning to wonder about it, where before, I just accepted it. Death, by its nature, can easily get you thinking crazy existentialist things and start running rings around your baser, more primitive feelings.

Two deaths on consecutive afternoons; it jolts even me out of my hard, callous, emotionless, cynical self.

The first visit - the call the day before - comes in just after five in the afternoon. It is fair to say that I hate late calls. I have done this job for a few years - a family doctor in Wormbridge - and I know already that I hate late calls. The worst thing is I know that this job will probably last until I retire (twenty, thirty years), and I already hate some parts of it. My contract is up for renewal in 2 months. Maybe then I will negotiate myself out of having to leave the surgery in the afternoon. And a few other parts that I won't bore you with.

Five o'clock and Wormbridge itself is beginning to wind down from its less than hectic day. It is a town on its knees and slowly dying itself.

The call comes in and it sounds innocuous enough but my jaw stiffens with the injustice. At least when the police call that next day there is still a tiny frisson of excitement, although usually it is some routine matter where they just need my scrawl on a piece of paper.

This call though, the day before Paul's death, is quite different.

## Smallpox Hill

Driving through Wormbridge to the man's house, I pass O'Sullivan's where there is a very special offer on a Flymo mower, and outside a traffic warden talks to an old man with a stick. The traffic warden rolls back and forward on her new black Dr. Marten soles. The town seems a prosperous place for traffic wardens; there are two or three of them. I smile at her. We are both part of this. The lady from The Hard Yards is closing up, a bag on her shoulder. Her shop is filled with hanks of material, lined up like rocket launchers. Three smart office women from the Valley Building Society talk at the mock Dickensian door to the office, which they have just locked. There is new gaudy paint on the front of the Cossack pub, down Pickering Lane. Around the town is a ghostly taste of previous bustle, now gone. I have chosen to spend the rest of my life looking after the dwindling population of this dwindling little market town. And then I think I must get the brakes fixed on this new car. It's a Skoda Octavia. I dislike it already and in secret hanker after my old Peugeot, now stacked crudely down at Alan's on the Bristol road. There is a grind the front wheel makes when I come to the cross-roads at the foot of Limcombe Hill. Perhaps, afterwards, I should sprint up to the top of that hill, survey my empire, see if I can glimpse the Severn down at Ardley and try and rid myself of this entrapped feeling, this feeling of being a puppet on which two thousand people have strings.

I know I won't because I never do.

All through this doctoring, I'm trying just to be clear and categorical, like medical textbooks are.

The man who has called me has a hernia: he has a protrusion of gut through the wall of the abdomen. When they get stuck these hernias have to be operated on. It's simple and categorical. Its good to have some rules, and this is one of the rules. This, however, is not the strange thing about the call. This is not what unnerves me and perhaps explains why I act like I do later on, when Paul has died. As soon as I walk in to the old man's house he tells me. Doctor, he says, I'm about to die.

Now no one knows what is going to happen. Sometimes it's difficult enough to know what has happened already, let alone what is going to happen.

He is not very ill and I tell him that although he needs to go to the hospital, he isn't going to die. I mean, God, we are all going to die. But I tell him no he is not dying. This is a mistake.

I arrange the ambulance on the telephone. I look at him as I talk. He is an old man, over ninety. His body has become an invertebrate shell, while, beneath it, his flesh has shrunk away. He has a long beard and a dark face with wild eccentric white hair in sprouts over his scalp and piercing unfrightened eyes, like George Bernard Shaw in those Victorian pictures.

So then, at this moment, he suddenly dies. His head slumps forward and from his throat comes a horrible bovine grunt. I notice the single panel of gas fire showing blue through the chrome bars and above it an electric beam swirls one way and then another in an extremely poor imitation of fire.

There is a peculiar way, at these moments, in

which time moves as an elongated, protracted thing. I call to his wife to help me. She is standing behind the door, her hands clasped, as though she were a dancer and these were the final moments before she was due to make her entrance. She is thin and she now starts wringing her hands. I physically manoeuvre her into a position so she can hold his head. She instinctual strokes his hair. It's a useless action which is entirely the right thing to do. We both know that there's no point trying anything. A good death is really what we all crave, and this is good enough, in his wife's arms in his own sitting room. In fact it doesn't really get any better.

So it is a kind of success.

But it nags at me. I am thinking over and over, how had he known? Medically there is no reason for him to die, and yet he has known it all along. What had brought him to that knowing? This is the part that unnerves me. It's the first time in years that I feel I really don't know what's going on. That life is more complicated and mysterious than I have given it credit for.

So, the very next afternoon, the police call, and I swear a bit inwardly, I suppose, because I lack any control over what is asked of me. And two in a row is bad luck. Then sometimes I think there is no such thing as bad luck, it's just that your life is set out wrong.

I go all the same. I'm just a bag of moans, except it's all inside, and I do what anyone asks in the end, in my servile way.

Paul is slumped on his bed. I know it's going to

be Paul because the Police have told me. I'm ready for that shock.

I park up behind the Mercedes, next to the house in Queen's Hill. I certified the addict in this very flat and now I'm about to consign Paul to the officially dead.

The wet May weather has left a stain under the Mercedes, of leaking oil. The hedge next to where the car is parked hangs down like a badly fitting curtain: over abundant, lying chaotically on the floor. There are little bits of rubbish that have blown in and caught in its branches and prickles so that it resembles a Christmas tree of sorts. The light is turning almost sickly yellow.

Some days I feel like I just don't deserve all that they throw at me. Perhaps they are relying on me too much, all these people. I am, in a way, angry. I feel enslaved. With all this selfish angst acting itself out within me, it is only later that I come to wonder, if Paul has done this to himself, then how and why?

The police are always a bit know-it-all on these occasions, and even they irritate me today. They say that the radio was playing when they found him and they haven't turned it off. Never change anything at the scene of a possible crime and all death is suspicious, after all.

Any medical history, they ask me, and I shake my head. I've been through this man's notes very recently. There is no reason for him to die. The younger officer is all testosterone and long inelegant fingers. His senior is a woman who's a bit more laid back. She is sort of transcendent.

"Can I have a look?" I ask them.

"As long as you don't move anything."

I've been to plenty of deaths before and this younger cop is beginning to piss me off. If anything, my absolute speciality is in death. It's just that they're mostly old folks, like the one yesterday. Paul is forty.

The Sugar Babes are singing *Push the Button* and the hollow sound of pop music gives the scene an alien, surreal atmosphere, as though we are on a stage set. Nothing is quite right. The light has taken on an even more malignant yellow.

"Have you found anything officer?" I ask the woman. I am not even going to talk to the man.

There has apparently been no sign of a struggle, no obvious wounds, no note or empty pill pot, no nothing in fact.

"He wasn't the suicidal type," I tell her.

"You know him then?" she asks. She's a bit kind of accusatory as well.

"Well, nearly," I say. She asks me what nearly means, but I don't answer. I'm looking at Paul, lying peaceful on the bed.

In life he was, if anything, much more grotesque. His body in death is slimmer and has a slightly hollow still beauty that, in life, he never really possessed.

His eyes are still open. He is actually completely cold. Because he is facing the wall the examination is actually rather difficult. It is obvious he is dead but still I have to shine a light in his eye and then listen pathetically to his heart which is of course completely silent. To do this I have to kneel on the bed and stretch around him to get access to his front. It is ungainly and slightly unbalanced. The young policeman looks as though he is all ready to come and haul me off. Paul has had a radical haircut since I last saw him. His face is bunched up on the bed, like he has gone to sleep, so that I never really see him as Paul. He is just another dead body and I must go through the pathetic motions. I don't even really look at his face because its facing the wall, only his eyes. Do his eyes react to light? Is there any notions working in his brain. These are the rules and at the moment I follow rules. Like I said, I need to be categorical.

A man walks along the pavement who has nothing to do with this situation but I notice him out of the window because he is dressed strangely, I must stop looking at these peripheral things in life and learn to concentrate more. The only way to describe him is to say that he looks like a left over from a sixties music happening circa *His Satanic Majesty Presents*. Faded felt robes like a medieval man, outrageous colour but all slightly going to seed. I think of weeds and flowers and being in the right place, or the wrong place. I also notice that you can see Smallpox Hill from here, from an odd angle that makes it look different to how I know it. I wish I was on top of that hill right now with Rosie drinking wine. And not here with a couple of rather unpleasant policemen and a dead body.

Paul is lying like he's just been reading, felt ill, stopped, and then died. Did he know he was going to die as well? Do we all get a premonition?

Usually with these sorts of visits I am all direction, callousness and, most of all, speed. Get things done and signed and get out as quickly as possible. I'm different with Paul.

Maybe it's just a selfish thing. I'm already trying to imagine the canyons that Maria will carve in her arms now, and the chaos that this finished life will cause Bernard. But I'm also intrigued, I have to admit. It's just not usual for a forty year old to drop down dead. I've seen it once or twice and it's usually a disease of the cardiac muscle. It's just from what Maria told me, I suppose: all that business that went on before. Is there some other reason why Paul is dead?

The light suddenly changes to a more healthy white sunlight. The two police officers are scribbling down stuff and also talking into radios. Why do they not use mobiles like the rest of us? Perhaps they don't make mobiles big enough for important policemen.

If Paul did just die, did he snort horribly like the man yesterday, or was it sudden and irrevocable?

A new song has come on the radio. It's something I don't recognise, but it's cheap and tasteless trance with no soul.

"Can I turn the radio off?" I ask the two police constables.

The younger man doesn't know what to say, the older woman says: "No, better not, not till the SOCO gets here."

"How about just turning it down, then," I say. "I can't stand this one."

They shake their heads. It's one of those jobsworth moments. Police have not been taught to be individuals; there is no individual responsibility, except to do exactly what the rest of the team are doing. They like everything categorical. Like me I suppose. I just choose when to be categorical.

So I carry on looking Paul over, as I'm allowed to do, with this dreary inappropriate inarticulate rave music filling up the bedroom. It's not his dead body that makes me flinch; death is all the same to me. There is something that is just not right. Paul has been wrapped up in all this dodgy company for years, but Maria says he's changed now, that he was becoming the family man, looking after Bernard and her. It sounds as if Paul has changed. He's given up the dodgy stuff. That was why he wanted the life assurance: he wanted to look after her. At forty, it's possible to change, if we really want to. It's just difficult to do, that's all.

"Can't we just turn the radio down, and then maybe turn it up when the SOCOs come."

I am pleading with them. Perhaps the actual volume is somehow significant in solving the mystery. They shake their heads and the younger, fuelled up one reminds me in his condescending way that I mustn't touch anything. I know that and I'm beginning to feel that if he tells me anything else I already know then something slightly unpleasant might happen between us.

I try and keep the music out of my head. Maybe it's because I don't have any brothers or sisters but I find it difficult to think when there's other noise or people talking. I feel a little muddled. I feel like this is not quite right.

He had been mixed up with some pretty low-life individuals, had Paul. He was not squeaky clean, by anyone's estimation. That's the first thing, even if Maria is right about him straightening out.

The second is that he's just applied for life assurance and I'm pretty certain he got it, judging by the medical report I gave, which was empty.

The third thing is he's just come back from Chiapas in Mexico.

The fourth thing is...now my head is getting pretty confused. Is there a fourth thing? Yes, the fourth thing is he's dead, lying in his room, and there's no really good reason why.

All this doubles my interest at least. I look at his hands; the nicotine staining and the blunt chipped nails. His wrists has no wrist watch mark, its all pale. Sun tans must fade when you die. I hadn't really thought about it before.

There's something else I don't like about this and maybe it's all the wine I've drunk in my life, but I just can't think of it. Something that is not quite right. So I take an extra careful look at him because of...oh I don't know, Maria, myself, my own curiosity?

There is his smooth chest, his shaved head, and his loose jeans. There is no point undressing him and upsetting the SOCOs when they arrive. Above all I want an easy life. He is wearing Dr Martens, like the traffic warden, done up smart with a bow. His legs are stretched on the bed and dug deep into the duvet that he lies on, so it's difficult to see them. I feel his legs through his trousers. Why exactly I'm doing this I have no idea. His shoes I notice are tied up differently, and also the laces are new. These are not exactly important observations.

Police work always seems pretty obvious when it's Sherlock Holmes or Dagleish, but to me now, I have no idea where to start. Nothing means anything. There are too many details and I'm sure I'm not concentrating properly. Christ, anyway I'm a doctor. Another doctor will cut Paul open and decide why he died. My only role in all this is to say that he is dead, which I do.

"What time are you certifying the death, Doc?" The younger policeman looks at me hard, like he doesn't like me, which I'm sure is true, although it's possible that he doesn't like anyone, judging by his face. I'm in two minds whether to pull him up on calling me doc, but I decide that as little interaction as possible is the best solution.

"Now," I say, "put it down as 5.15 pm." Technically Paul dies at this point. I have said he is dead, and suddenly, in the eyes of the law, he is dead. Although he is facing the wall, its pretty clear there is no knife in his back or bullet wounds and I surmise that he probably just had something wrong with him that no body knew about and at least his death wasn't drawn out and agonising. So I just say he's dead, and then like I say, he dies.

You have no idea the power I have.

Or how often I get things wrong.

# CHAPTER FIVE

The next thing I hear about Paul is from the undertaker.

The undertakers in Wormbridge are an odd collection of people, just like almost everywhere else: they like their beer, they're tall and strong so that they can carry coffins, they can laugh and joke like people do around death, and as well as this, they can come on all sincere and heart felt sympathy and a soft touch of hand.

Justin Whatmore is like a prototype for undertakers. He's just going grey, a little, although I suspect he actually enhances this. He is handsome in the traditional sense, a full head of hair, neatly combed, a large full face, like an actors': well proportioned. His face works; it all fits together.

He's had a lot of girlfriends has Justin. People like him, he's well organized. They say that our perception of beauty is based on an averaging. The best looking amongst us, apparently, have a face that has no extremes, but has all features averaged from the population. When I see Justin I think of that. There's absolutely nothing wrong with him. It's all perfect.

This time he's got his sincere voice on, when he phones me, and I detect something else as well. His offices are down the other end of Wormbridge.

When I have to examine a body, I have to cross the road and unlock this shed-like building where, inside, the bodies lie, chaotic like they have fallen asleep at an all night party and someone has covered them up with a white sheet so they don't get cold, or in this case so they don't get warm. Even though I'm cold and heartless, this even scares me a little, even with the handsome Justin

It's not a cremation this time, Justin says. Usually he telephones me because for a cremation, he needs two doctors to examine the body. Just to be sure I suppose. But this time he is frankly worried.

Sometimes, at the moment, I feel like there is too much death about me, like I stink of it. I'm meant to be a doctor, for God's sake, keeping people alive. Rosie says she can tell: I get morose and start to not listen when she's talking. Last night, she took me up Limcombe Hill, like I've been promising to do to myself. It's May and the evening is loud and full and bursting with life and humidity. The dampness brings up the smell of the elderflower and the philadelphus that's sweet like the sea on the best of days. The hill itself looks like a slag heap grown over with grass. It's perfectly conical for some odd geographical reason that was once explained to me but now I forget. It's a Volcano, I sometimes think when I drive past, and that sets me thinking that my life should really be called *Under the Volcano*, except that they roll the consul off the cliff at the end of that book, just like a dog. Our lives seem sort of dominated by this hill, which gives out views all over Wormbridge, across to Smallpox Hill, down to the Severn at Ardley and past to the Nuclear power station that, for some reason, in that instant, is caught by a low aberrant ray of orange sun, and instead of the grey concrete of its silos, or whatever they are called, the whole building is glowing like a wonderful piece of lava.

When we get to the top, I'm out of breath. I am unfit and I breathe and breathe well past Rosie's recovery. I have a job where I sit and chat all day. Rosie is constantly doing stuff. She walks for miles, does Rosie. Her arms are brown and strong. She thinks in odd and lovely spirals. Sometimes what she says seems so profound and honest. It is chilling like very, very cold water. It suddenly illuminates areas that have never been explored.

At the top we sit down and then I lay my head in her lap. We are in love after all and this is what lovers do. She tells me that I am tense, that I need to relax.

At some points in my life I have felt that I don't need anyone. That I'm unattached because I am strong and don't need attachments. I like to be on my own and make my own decisions. The difficult part for me is that I need Rosie. I need her earthy reason. I need her lap to lie my head in and her hands to smooth out my forehead. I look up at her and her hair is rich and red and falls down over her shoulders. Her face has a texture of, oh I don't know, maybe sand and something else more luscious. The best things are impossible to describe.

I tell Rosie everything. I always tell her everything. I'm not meant to and she knows that and she never is anything but careful. After all, I have to tell someone, I can't keep everything that I see inside. I'd go mad well before two months is up and I get my new contract. I tell her about the addict upstairs, above Maria, who a month after she's met Paul, dies quietly of an overdose because of some new gear coming in from Africa. I tell her about how Paul gets the house and how happy I feel, not about the death but just for Maria. We all need some luck, after all. I tell her that a month later Paul is dead so what sort of luck is that. Then we fall silent and almost immediately, as though miracles do happen, the deep red May sun at 9pm manages to slip out like a spilt fruit beneath the clouds and floods Limcombe Hill and Smallpox with its red light. We both sit up and enjoy it on our faces. Sometimes nothing needs to be said.

We walk down the hill again. The heat from the day's sun lifts itself to my face. I feel better but also I feel a bit confused. Rosie does this to me. It's always been confusing, right from the beginning. I want her and then sometimes I don't want her: I feel stifled by her, as though she is holding me back. From what I never really find out. So now, after three years, I feel like I owe her something, that I shouldn't just split with her because that would be unfair. A betrayal. There would be something immoral about it. Also, I adore her and need her.

Her body is warm and when I feel that warmth I know there is something human which I need from Rosie. It's not sex or anything like that. It's her body, her livingness.

So, walking down the hill after the sun has set, I'm slightly confused and I'm attached and I feel better too.

But it's not really enough preparation for what Justin is about to tell me.

He comes on the phone flustered like I haven't known him before. That's one thing about being an undertaker: death is a definite thing, there is no real risk, not until today. No decisions really only a bowed head and some kind words.

"She's taken the body back to her house!" he says.

There is a pause and then I say, "Well?"

"Well, it's just not right. I've been at this job for fifteen years and I'm just not happy about this."

"What's not right about it Justin? Now the post mortem is done, don't next of kin have a right to have the body in the house? The Welsh lay them out in the front parlour, don't they? It's not illegal."

Justin sounds really out of sorts: the oak honed voice of his is missing the normal deep consonants.

"It's her, I suppose. She seems out of control."

Another pause. I can't believe that this man, this fellow professional is about to dump this one on me. He knows by calling that he is handing responsibility on to me.

"Like how?" I ask. I'm good at keeping people at bay simply by asking questions.

"She wailing a lot, she's screaming, she's...I don't know, talking to him weirdly like he's still alive. She was mumbling something to him about joining him. I don't know but I think she might top herself. She's out of control. That's what I mean, she's not safe. I think we will have to take the body back."

I take a deep breath. Above all else in this job you have to be flexible. Now deep down I harbour a slight grudge against Justin, something I barely know myself. It's something about his good looks and how he gets lots of women and his suave manner. I don't want to be anything like him, God no, but I sort of envy him and at this moment maybe that gets in the way. You have to keep your personal feelings out of situations like this, but I want to rant at him and belittle him on how he knows so little about what real life is like, and about all the freaks that inhabit the world, not just the dolled up ones who go to theme nights at the The Oak, the pub on the corner where Justin does most of his picking up.

"That woman has gone through a hellish life, Justin. You wouldn't believe what her arms look like. You won't believe all the fucked up things that have happened to her. Then two months ago, she meets a man, a man that, I don't know, maybe she's fallen in love with, or whatever. You know what I mean. She is happy for the first time since she was a child. A month later, when the addict dies upstairs, he moves in and they make it into one house, a proper home, and Maria gives it a go at playing normal life. I have watched her blossoming, Justin, it's been wonderful. Then, he dies. Just like that. No warning, just dies. The Police take him off, the pathologist cuts him up, he is returned; she wants him back. You know about grieving Justin, you must be an expert on grief. She doesn't believe he is dead, she is numb from the shock; this is searching Justin. Can't you just let her have her few moments with the only good person she's ever met?"

I go on sometimes, it's getting worse as I get older. All men seem to be the same in this respect. Perhaps I've said too much, and I've sworn as well, but hell, that's what needs to be said, after all.

"It's just the suicide bit that worries me," he continues. "You should have seen her, she was well out of control. It's just I've never seen anything like it."

"So," I answer, "you think I need to assess her?"

"Yes…Yes I do." Justin often repeats himself, for extra gravitas I suppose.

I take the phone away from my ear. All that time with Rosie last night is ebbing away, just like time does: slips through your fingers without you being able to grab it and keep it. I look at the phone. I don't really know why I'm doing it. As though to check that this is real, what I am hearing is real.

Another late visit. I tell Justin I'll go at 7pm, after evening surgery. I'm all cheery and jocular with him. It's either that or I'll get angry. Sometimes being false is a good thing. Rosie says something about being honest: how in the end it's easier on the memory to be honest because there is less to remember. I think she's wrong. Sometimes it's great to be false. Especially with Justin the undertaker who really is made out of plastic when it comes to the falseness stakes. At least I'm way behind him.

The other doctor working that day is Sue, and Sue can't handle Maria. She's good is Sue; patients like her, she likes them, and she doesn't miss much. She's always polite. That's about all the good things I can think about her. Otherwise she's dull and pedantic.

You can see what a selfish bitch of a man I can become, but then, like Rosie said, I'm just being honest.

So it's me that will have to visit the mad and bereaved Maria. The receptionists grin inanely as I get them to find her notes. They are large notes, about the same as 6 peoples' notes put together. I sometimes think that this means that she has had six times as much life, but it doesn't work like that.

One of the receptionists treats me like she is my mum: pats me on the back sympathetically if it's all going wrong. Light comes through the window and grazes the computer screens. The waiting room is finally getting emptier. It's like some kind of market out there, people talking and waiting and worrying.

The receptionists are like my minders: they take the calls; they get most of the strop from people and then I am the white knight, keen and smiling and helping one and all. It's surprising they're not physically sick sometimes, the way the patients talk to them, or more like shout and then when they put me on, it's all sweetness and please and thank you doctor.

I feel for them. They're all intelligent women who, by dint of living in our society, have just got a job doing something worthwhile to keep them interested. They're surprisingly astute: Sheila, in particular, warns me sometimes about impending disasters and they keep an eye on what I do. We are a team, hard and driven. Tonight though - and this is where I'd rather be them than me - tonight, I have to visit Maria. They couldn't do it and frankly wouldn't want to. In the end, if all else fails there is me. I will be the one trying to decide whether Maria is about to successfully kill herself.

Three late visits in one week, and three weird ones at that. Maybe what I said about bad luck is just wrong. How many episodes of bad luck prove that it can't happen by chance? When will I know it's just me?

So I'm driving down the dead streets of Wormbridge again. The weather has come on all hot, the clouds build up in silver until the silver becomes so much it turns to grey, greasy grey. There is going to be a storm, you can just feel it; the wind blows irregularly and it so hot - hot Saharan wind - it can't possible stay this hot and not rain. The world is too much of an unstable place for that.

Kids are waiting out on street corners, sitting, hang dog in the heat.

I get out next to Maria's house. One of the kids I know because his Mum brings him in regularly. He conceals a cigarette behind his back and then says hello and then spoils it all by calling me Doc. I grimace inwardly. I do a lot of stuff inwardly. Rather than a portrait in the attic like Dorian Gray, I just have extremely ugly insides, if you could see them.

The front garden still has the upturned pram although it's been pushed to the side and the grass is cut. They built these houses in 1940 for some Canadian air force personnel and they were going to knock them down after the war. This is about the only one with two floors, the rest are bungalows

If I had nerves before, they are all gone now. I'm expecting something bizarre and I'm ready for it. I've done this job long enough now.

"Why are *you* here?" She speaks in a partial snarl. Sometimes you can see the animal in Maria: it's closer to the surface than with most of us. She is suspicious, and that involves - like a dog would do - coming on all-aggressive.

"Justin Whatmore rang me, the Undertaker, they were worried about you."

It suddenly seems to occur to her that I may be there to reclaim Paul: sort of section him and carry him away. It's like social workers and children. I am, for the first time with Maria, seen as a threat and an enemy.

She clams up all hard. Her lips which are normally so full become thin and withdrawn. This is going to be difficult, this is going to take all my skill, just to get into the house, let alone in some way help her. She doesn't look like she's in the mood for help.

But then, she doesn't look actively suicidal either. Three quarters of me thinks that a quick chat about killing oneself and I could be home in ten minutes, write up my assessment and go around to Rosie's and have a deep hot bath with some of her expensive bath oil.

## Smallpox Hill

The other quarter of me is the problem. The part that is screaming in my ear that Paul's death is somehow wrong and one more look at his body may, I don't know, reveal the base of this little mystery. Then I remember the fifth thing, the missing part, the doubt I couldn't remember at the scene of the crime. It came to me when I pressed Maria door bell. Push the Button, The Sugar Babes and the radio and that up tight police constable who wouldn't let me turn it off. That's what I couldn't think of.

Paul hated the radio.

## CHAPTER SIX

What I always forget with Maria is that she plays killdeer. She cannot help but play, because she has had to play all her life. If you remember that, then there is a chance at least that you can help her. After I've spent five minutes haggling with Maria on her doorstep I manage to convince her that I am not about to take Paul away from her again, but I need to talk. It takes a while to get her to trust me, to let me inside.

Maria is dressed all sassy and smart. I've never seen her so dressed up. Apart from her eyes, that are nearly closed, she looks as though she might be going out on a Friday night: she's done her face and made the most of her not inconsiderable beauty. What she's playing at the moment is 'lead them away from Paul, they are not having him back.' She's doing this by pretending to be suicidal so that the emphasis is back on her, and we stop concentrating on Paul. She is leading us away from what she loves the most, using her own wounds, like a bird might limp and feign injury: lure the hunters away from her treasure.

Justin sort of fell for it, but it backfired and although she is a master, you have to know whom you are up against. Justin is a control freak: he just wants everything as it should be, no funny business.

Maria, I know immediately, is no more suicidal than she's ever been. Maria is deeply flawed because her life, this far, has taught her all sorts of weird lessons, one of which is that if you say you want to die, everyone comes running; they chase you. It's like saying boo to a hunter and then scurrying off.

So that's how I get in: by showing her I have no interest in her special treasure, no interest in taking this from her.

I tell her pretty much straight away. I say, "I'm not here to take Paul away; he's yours until you bury him." Then I say, "I've come to see you, I'm just worried about you."

She looks at me in that way of hers: without trust, scrutable, half eyed. Am I now playing a game? Who is playing what?

"You're jus' like the others, you jus' want to cart me off don't you?" Something in her recent medication - or is it her mental state? - does not allow her to say her Ts.

I shake my head but I stay silent.

"Jus' like the res' of them who say 'I think you need a bit of time to recover, you can't look after yourself Maria.'" She says this in a lisping babyish voice. "You're no' really interested in me, you're jus' covering yourself jus' in case I do top myself and then it would be your fault. It's your job, that's all, whereas this is my life."

I still manage to stay silent. Being silent is about the best thing I do as a doctor. It gets me out of all types of tricky situations.

"You reckon you're differen' and I thought you were for a long time but now I know your just another fucking doctor doing his job."

She's going on the attack to lead the situation away from her treasure who lies dead next door. Again it is important to say nothing. I'm not about to start defending myself. It's nothing to me. She's trying to personalise all this and I need to keep myself out of it, for as long as possible.

I'm still standing at the door and the pushchair is behind me and tipped over.

"Where's Bernard, anyway?" I say. That pushchair makes me think of him and the tablets.

"He's gone away, staying with Mum."

I'm not getting far at all. Perhaps, having seen Maria, like I said, I could call this a sort of assessment and then just leave and trust that she doesn't kill herself and if she does, what can I do anyway? I suppose I could section her and get her carted into the secure bit of The Royal Hospital, but what really is the point of that? It would just add a sort of unconsummated grief into her already complex mental makeup. She needs to grieve for this man, in which ever way she chooses, otherwise there really is no help.

Then I try a more daring move. I ask her when she's going to make me a cup of tea. She raises up her shoulders and pulls down her short skirt by holding onto the hem and tugging. Then she sighs and motions me inside.

The house is cramped. The stairs, now opened up since they had been sharing the upstairs and downstairs flats, end almost exactly where we step inside the front door. In behind the stairs is a door to the kitchen that she leads me through. Some newly installed French windows lead out onto a patio area where all the weeds, almost everything in fact, has been killed by some sort of spray and now the only colour is the limp yellow foliage and the puckered grey of the concrete slabs. Now there's a tidy garden.

The table has a pub ashtray over-flowing with butts. The sink is surprisingly clear and clean. In a strange way, I've never seen Maria so sorted: she has a direction of a kind; she is busy around the house while the kettle boils. She is aware. That's what it is, usually she is not aware, not even of herself and now she is aware of herself and of her house.

When the kettle boils she makes tea and sets two cups on the table. She sweeps away the ashtray, empties it, washes it, resets it on the table next to the cups, sits down and lights a cigarette.

Then she looks up at me.

"Do you mind?" she says although I'm really not sure she would put it out if I said that yes I did. For the first time in three years I think, with a pang, that I'd like a cigarette too. Rosie hates me smoking, I gave up for her and I feel cured, until right now anyway.

I watch Maria smoking. I've never seen her actually smoke, only smelt her and seen her fingers. She devours cigarettes as though they really are very important. It is not an idle thing, her smoking.

We don't say anything when we drink the tea. Then I ask if the post mortem has been reported: if they know why he died. This might seem blunt, but I have learnt that its no use pretending someone is not dead when they are. And anyway, I know for certain that Maria was not thinking of anything else but the dead body that was lying out in her house.

She hasn't heard anything.

There is a long, long silence next and I stare into my tea. I'm not sure quite what I'm trying to achieve by all this. Some support I suppose and a bit of assessment. I tell her that when someone of his age dies all of a sudden, it's usually something wrong with his heart. She nods but she is not interested because it's not going to make him not dead even if we agree on why he died.

So we lapse back into silence.

This is the strange thing: in so many ways I've never seen Maria so well organised. She has lost probably the one person she has properly loved, who has equally loved her back and she is on the top of her game. Often these most perverse reversals happen, as though there is something in human nature that procures a survival of sorts. God only knows why Maria is like this, but I'm beginning to feel I'm glad I've come: glad, almost elated.

I look at Maria. She has no idea that she is ill in any way. It is only that she has this pain. She has tears running down her face and I really don't know why I do this but I reach out and take her in my arms. There is no sense of lust or taking advantage. There is no sense of anything apart from it feels like this is what I should do; this is what humans do when one is feeling desperate. She grips on to me hard and presses her whole body in to me and sobs and shakes like her body is convulsing. I hug her tighter and suddenly I feel confused and light headed and dizzy with a feeling that I don't recognise.

Quite suddenly she says she has to go upstairs and leaves me to her smouldering cigarette. For a minute or so I sit and stare at it burning down and then for no reason that I can clearly think of, I take a drag and then put it out. I really don't know why I do what I do next and thinking back to it I wonder if it's all down to the evil of tobacco. It's amazing the excuses you can come up with. I decide I want to see Paul one last time, before he is buried. There are one or two issues I'm quite keen to get straight in my mind about Paul.

I open the door beyond the stairs. There are only candles lit, no daylight. The coffin has been placed on top of a shorter table so that his head and shoulders, and his feet and lower legs have become suspended, unsupported, like something in ballet. He is dressed very smoothly: white Fred Perry shirt, the top two buttons undone; Chinos, black leather shoes, shined up. His face is covered up with a white piece of material made from lace. As before, I am struck by the unnatural beauty of his body, which, in life, he did not possess. A slightly hollow, still, beauty.

It is inevitable that when a man your own age dies, you think of your own death. I am used to the older people, like the man who knew he was about to die, like so many people I see, but Paul is young; he shouldn't be dead any more than me. The only other person of my age who I have seen dead, had hung herself. The thought creeps up on me that maybe Paul did this to himself, but then there is no motive. Any act of violence - and suicide is the most violent of deaths - has to have a motive.

I then think about Maria upstairs. The strange thing is, through all the bohemian artistic people that I hang out with who think they are avant-garde or philosophers, none have this passion for survival: a type of angry survival that grips her in its stead. She is the strangest of people but strong and different and complicated.

I look long at Paul with his head covered. There doesn't seem to be anything else to do in this room. There are two candles to the side of the coffin. I notice two things: first his hands and second the silence. The latter is absolute; the world is muffled, wrapped up, against, I'm not sure, wind and unkindness. I don't like the silence.

I carry on looking at him for some time. I'm really thinking how I can get out now: escape back to my normal life, away from this situation, ease myself away without upsetting Maria.

There's just one thing I want to check for myself. It's just one of those stupid things: it was the shoelaces I suppose. I just would like to have a look at his feet. Can I really just take his shoes and socks off? What if Maria comes back in? I'm not sure about Maria: I'm not at all sure how she will react. There's this ownership thing going on, she's unstable and hopelessly out of control really. But I suppose I'm just a bit bullish: I tramp into people lives like I have a right to do it. So I quickly untie his buffed up shoes and slip off his socks. I am looking carefully when with a sort of dread I hear the door handle turn.

"What the fuck are you doing?" she says.

She rips the socks and shoes from my hands and starts to carefully put them back again. She is muttering madly to herself and her lips are moving and screwed up. She glares at me like she hates me, which I have every reason to believe she does. She is crying as well.

"You fucking doctors have already cut him up and had a look inside, haven't you done enough? Can't you keep your filthy fucking fingers off him?"

It's as though I've cheated her. I've got to her preciousness saying I'm not interested and then been caught red handed. All that careful nurturing, all that proper care and attention I've lavished on her, all the trust we've made together, our whole relationship is pretty much destroyed.

I say I'm sorry. Then she starts screaming. She loses it really badly when she loses it, does Maria. I remember her telling me about some incident on a bus when a man tried to put his hand down her bra. She said then how she screamed her head off and in the end the bus driver just had to force her off the bus. It's like her anger is water hemmed in by a dam and when something breaches that dam, the water pours out, faster and faster and more furious, and there's no way of putting it back where it comes from or ever hoping to stop it, until it runs dry.

So, in the end, I just leave. I realise I've cocked this one up, badly. Sometimes things come out better than you expect; sometimes they don't. What I regret is that I feel like I might have been able to help Maria in the next few weeks, properly help her into bereavement. That and a feeling I've let us down, I've destroyed something. I know she has no one, apart from the Stanley knife and the pill packet. I suppose as well I pride myself on the fact that I can handle Maria: she likes me and listens to me, and she despises other doctors. It's part of my conceited view of the world. My deception of myself is being found out, the secret which I do not allow any others to see, and now they know it's there, it won't be long before I realise my whole life is built on a fallacy. That I'm good and kind and try and help people, and that people can talk to me and they find they feel better if they talk to me, because basically I'm a good person. Except now I know I don't really care about Maria, it's the fact that she cares about me that's important.

Why Maria's outburst should affect me like this I don't know. Maybe the doubts were building up anyway. After all, I can't continue lying to myself for ever. Maybe it's just Maria's high pitched yelling as I close the door that shatters something fragile within me. Patients aren't really allowed to yell at me like this: it's against some unwritten rule.

In my haste to get away I trip over the upturned pushchair where Bernard hides this fucking woman's medicine. I swear loudly and unprofessionally. In the car I stop at the Co-op on the way back home, buy some cigarettes and then drive to Wormbridge Peak car park where, allegedly, you can watch people having sex in cars. I look out over the view. It's what people call a beauty spot, but it's only beautiful if you look west: behind you is the big car park where my Skoda Octavia creaks and groans as it cools down. The sun is out again but it's more silver in the haze, like an etched glass blanket. I smoke but it's not really what I want. I think long and hard. Thoughts are most like smoke: the way they evolve and change. I need to make a few changes; I need to sort myself out. Too much philosophy, too many philosophical friends seem to have cocooned me from the real world, from real animal-like passions. Perhaps that's a good thing. I need to immerse myself not in philosophy but in the landscape, the majesty of the hills, the eeriness of being alone within nature.

I sometimes have moments such as these and I know that they'll pass.

There is some ugly agricultural sound down in Herdlsey where the hill flattens out like a tablecloth that tips towards the estuary of the Severn and onwards to the Forest of Dean; a distant country where the Romans never fully subjugated the mad Celts. There is an absolute dryness to the fields and even the grey sands of the estuary. The landscape seems almost shrunken and obsolete in the heat. May Hill stands forlorn and the Brecon Beacons rise like bubbles in a pond, disappearing with the curve that the earth makes.

I become aware that the landscape is sort of

hiding us within in it. There are so many small dramas and excitements hidden behind doors and windows, so many stories unfolding themselves, so much yearning, which no one can see. It's just I can see: I can see into one of those windows a bit more clearly than I would like. That's why I need the landscape back. I need to step away from all this detail and wallow in all this unchallenged beauty.

I need to forget, too, what I have seen on Paul's right foot. It's only going to make everything more complicated. The tiny little mark just above and behind his big toe. God and that radio business as well, and all the other strange shit that's swirling around me.

It's raining heavily by the time I am driving home. The storm that has been brewing has finally boiled up completely. The brakes squeal again, as I turn down Pickering Lane. I must get them fixed, I say again, but it's already just another thing I've got to fix. Things are mounting up around me. I'm more confused by the day: there's Rosie, that's confusing; there's my new contract coming; there's my whole life rolled out in front of me and not really looking very exciting; there's Paul who's dead and there's Maria who's acting up; there's Sue at the surgery who, in reality, doesn't pull her weight; there's red wine of which I'm drinking too much. There's all sorts of rubbish cluttering up my life. I need a holiday. I need to get to the sea and smell that salt water and the coconut gorse and see that colour blue.

And I need to know who would want Paul dead and why they would kill him like that, just after he's got his life insurance set up. Was that benevolent chance or is there something much, much more malignant going on?

So many things to know.

When I get home there is a note on the door. Its Rosie's handwriting, 'We need to talk,' it says.

## CHAPTER SEVEN

The strange thing about memory, what the neurology text books never tell you, is that in fact its easier to remember than it is to forget. For a week now I have not thought too much about Paul and how he might have died. There's plenty going on at the surgery that keeps me from it. And plenty at home as well.

I see Rosie that next night and she gives me a sort of ultimatum. For some reason I'm clutching her hasty written note when I walk up to her house, like it's got a question on it that I don't want to forget to answer. We need to talk, but actually what happens is she needs to talk and to tell me exactly how crap I am. Her house is this odd dark red brick affair tucked into the woods at the top of the field. One thing I love about Rosie is her house. Maybe it's because Rosie lives there, although this time, Rosie living there doesn't really do anything for me. I am a crap partner I suppose: I don't really give

Rosie what she wants. I'm not even quite sure what it is she wants: fun? I don't know, beauty? Love perhaps, companionship. She tells me that I don't give her enough support; it's always the other way round and she is fed up.

I tell her it's just bad at work at the moment, and then she starts crying and says I need a new job. I hug her and then we both cry because…because, well it isn't good any more and we both know that.

Rosie comes from an alternative family. Her childhood, she says, was full of art and music, full of foreigners with strange ideas. Her father was a super patriarch who ruled his family with a strong iron fist. He was large with big arms and he was ripe for hugging. There was a sort of free love thing going on, free as long as he approved. Her friends envied her those exotic people who sat in her kitchen on most nights and the wild parties. She, though, ran away in the end and hitched up with a marketing man, and then after that (God forbid!), a doctor: the purveyor of pills and injections, the anathema to her upbringing. Rejection is difficult for those who have rebellious parents. It becomes a double negative so that we embrace what most others embrace. Sometimes, Rosie says, it's good to be normal. I am normal although I have always wanted to be a little bit unusual. My dad was maddeningly normal and dull and I hated it. There's always that playfulness in God, or whoever is controlling things up there.

So, at the end, Rosie, who has separated herself from most of her family, says that she wants me, no, she needs me how I was. That's my ultimatum.

Days later I am trying to develop all sorts of

games to stop me thinking. I become an avid reader; I fill any spare evenings with DVDs or trips down the M5 to Cribbs Causeway to catch some mindless movie. I phone Rosie lots and I can feel it coming easier, but she doesn't want me to come around. I play football on the hard court at the secondary school with a bunch of miscellaneous misfits who I fit in with well. I drink at the pub in the village and talk to any one I want. I think of Rosie, but there is something up with Rosie and I'm not sure what I'm doing. She says to me one night that I am cold and I don't have real friends. She may be right but I like to think that men make friends in different ways. I've two or three friends down in Bristol, people I like. They're the philosophers and sometimes I tire of them. One teaches at the university and is going out with an ex student which I think he feels is pretty clever. But I like these people.

I start getting up early: it's too hot to sleep and the mornings before work are like an oasis. The sky and atmosphere feels charged for the day. I walk for three or four miles, drink a smoothie for breakfast, survey the ashtray from the night before and the finished bottle of Rioja. My smoking is increasing like I knew it would. Mark the postman brings in a pile of bills and some extra-special offer from Somerfields supermarket, which strangely has a special offer for said Rioja. There is also an invite to Justin's fortieth birthday bash, to be held at the Oak Tree pub and is fancy dress with a Madonna theme. Umm. Hand written is a little message that makes me wince: Rosie's invited as well.

I notice that the post-mortem report has come back about half way through the morning surgery. I'm late, there are four people waiting, so I hungrily leave it till afterwards. One of the four is Julian: Julian is twentyish; he is a friend of Maria's friend, I think. I'm not sure if she knew him before but she'll know him now, sure enough. He has moved into the empty flat above Maria. The stairs have been boarded up again, into two cupboards. He has a one-month contract, like Paul. How is anyone meant to keep going one month at a time?

Julian does nothing all day or rather he is nothing all day; he sits in his underpants, laptop on lap, talking idly to friends on Facebook. Sometimes he sells a few 'plans', a piece or two of dealing, here and there. Otherwise he is strangely worried about going out, oddly agoraphobic.

Julian exudes a sort of slacker charm: very urban, very now and very idle. He is not classically handsome or intelligent and tends to get lost a little when he tries to explain some rather over complicated point. He is like a surfer who doesn't surf. Square jawed, bad-moodish lips. He seems sort of retired and irretrievably old, even though he is only twenty-two. It is incredible that he does so little and smokes and drinks so much and manages to stay reasonably healthy. It is only the young that can be so inactive and neglectful of their bodies and remain healthy; it is part of the arrogance of youth.

He registered with me yesterday and as I talk to him I ask him about the flat. He tells me about the two dead flatmates before him and I tell him I knew them both. Does it worry him?

"No," he says.

Julian moves slowly. He even moves his lips slowly. He is tall and underdeveloped. He is chaotic, dirty and exotic. He seems to exist for no reason apart from his easy going-ness. His limbs are graceful and effortless.

I say, "Well, I suppose it's a good thing you're not superstitious. Some people would get freaked-out by moving in there."

I genuinely haven't thought about Paul or Maria for a week or so. I can blot things out like that. Rosie is right: I am cold, an automaton without emotions. But now this man, moving in above Maria, maybe sleeping in the same bed Paul has slept in. And that reminds me of that PM report burning away in my in tray.

"Oh no, I don't get freaked by that shit." He drawls and stretches out his vowels like an Australian.

"Have you ever been to Australia?" I ask him.

"No…no I got the dregs of this tan in Mexico, southern Mexico."

"Oh," I say, "so what were you doing down there, holiday?" I am a doctor, I can ask anything and most people give me a straight answer.

"Oh, just some business, for some friends of mine."

I look at him. Business is a dirty word to me anyway, and I'm not sure who would engage Julian in any sort of business at all. But maybe he is not what he seems. Rosie says I'm always labelling people before I really know them. It's just my hunch that Julian isn't that reliable and furthermore I'm pretty certain I'm right.

Life has a habit of producing clang associations. That's a medical term for when psychotic schizophrenic types find a word that could mean two partly appropriate things. It's crass language stuff that to the rest of us is petty and meaningless. To them however it seems like nearly blinding brilliance. So Julian, just like Paul before him, had been moved into the same flat and then had a holiday in Southern Mexico, Chiapas if we want to be fussy. It's like hearing a song you haven't heard on the radio for ages, then hearing again that same day. Maybe Rosie's right in an obtuse way: maybe I'm coming to be psychotic because to me this makes one big clang. Southern Mexico. Now plenty of people go to Cancun. I've no problem with that but Chiapas, maybe some students, some archaeology buffs, not Paul and Julian. I'm aware that you hear surprising things every day if you keep your ears open and once does not arouse anything in me, but twice.

It clangs horribly. Wake up, it seems to be saying, smell the coffee or get out of the kitchen. Mix up your metaphors as much as you like, but I could still not pick up the cue, it just clanged.

I see coincidence and clangs all over the place. All of this life can be like never ending repeats: patterns of life repeating again and again, repeating and repeating itself, first as tragedy then as farce and who knows maybe then as horror and then worst of all, indifference.

Anyway, I tell Julian that it's good to meet him.

It's a manner of speech but, as well, there seems nothing malevolent about him. He is not ill in any way and I doubt if I'll see him much.

He is relaxed when he gets out of the chair. His movements remind me of a man who has repeated a skill many times over; it is all economy and grace.

I race through the next three patients; it's hard on them because its not their fault I'm late, but I am late and in addition there is the small matter of the post-mortem report that's sitting in its brown A5 envelope in my tray. I rush from my room to the reception office. In the waiting room I notice a strange looking man in off-red velvet clothes: very odd and grand, clearly some sort of long-term psychiatric patient, and although I vaguely recognise him, I don't know him as a patient, yet. It can't be long though because the weirdos tend to gravitate to me in the end. Sue never has enough time for them. He gets up as if to speak to me, but I motion with my eyes that I'm not available to talk to. I just want to have a look at that post-mortem report and things keep trying to stop me. Later I wish I had spoken to him: it would have helped him and me.

Sheila in reception gives me a broad smile and asks me how the morning was. I tell her about the PM report that's sitting in my tray and she says she noticed that.

"Should make some interesting reading," she says and she touches my arm. She's actually much more affectionate than my own Mum ever is. She looks after all of us, does Sheila, as though she has the biggest heart in Wormbridge, with room for us all in its ventricles. She knows I've been waiting for this one: she picks up when something is getting to me, does Sheila, and this one has certainly got right into me. Usually I open these things with her; she reads them if she wants before they get filed anyway, it sort of shares the burden and this doctoring can be a lonely business. It's good to have company.

This time however, I take the whole of my tray to my room.

The report is over about four pages. It always is. It reminds me of a school report because they have to say sort of standard things: 168 cm Caucasian male, general description, my name because I officially said he was dead and I was his GP until that moment, a quick mention of any past medical problems, of which there aren't in this case, and then a thorough trawl through each of Paul's bodily systems. It's written in a dry, scientific way and is extremely dull to read. For a closing chapter in someone's life book, it's pretty grim and would discourage any sequels if it were a bestseller. But it signals the last testament of Paul.

It's all too much to read and I notice the pulps of my fingers are slightly damp with an unheralded excitement. So I turn to the last page because I know there will be a summary: a quick route to finding out how someone killed Paul. What it says shocks me, and I read it three times.

Now death is always mediated in the end, by the heart stopping. No matter what it is that kills you, it's the heart stopping that is the final act. It's what causes the heart to stop that is interesting, not the fact that the heart stops. So this is what is shocking: according to the report, nothing has stopped Paul's heart, it just stopped. There is nothing wrong with his heart, in fact the pathologist comments on the low level of atherosclerosis and cholesterol deposits for a man of his age. So Paul just died and there was no cause.

I read the whole bloody report in the end; there is nothing in it. Paul is normal and healthy, he is like me, except that he is dead and I am not. There is no comment about what I've seen on Paul's feet, this was clearly not noticed but then again there was only a tiny mark and that was exactly what I was looking for. Finding things are much easier if you have an inkling of where to look.

I sit back in my chair. In retrospect I realise that this is the moment at which I could change what happens next: I could have aborted this whole thing, taken the ejector seat option and let things be; gone back to being how I was before Paul had died or even turned up in Wormbridge. I am at another cairn piled high with rocks. I am about to take things past the point of no return. Except that, at this moment, I don't know anything properly and there is something complicated that compels me down this path. After all, it is extremely unusual to act free of any perceived compulsions: we are channelled into paths like we are needles on a record.

So I pick up the phone and call the pathology department. The pathologist who did this post mortem is not the regular one but someone the police occasionally use. I've not heard of this one before, but I tell the receptionist that yes, it is quite urgent, he's due to be buried tomorrow and I want to chat through a few things. She gives me his mobile number and I ring it.

The man who answers has an extremely arrogant manner; he is posh to the point of stiffness. They say about pathology, that it is a profession for people who train as doctors but suddenly realise that they don't like people at all. Well, not living ones anyway. They often have difficult or awkward ways of communicating, which goes some way to explaining those awful reports that they issue, or maybe that's a legal thing.

I tell him my name and he repeats it, "Dr Nicholas Bradley, I can't say I've heard of you before."

"Actually its Dr Bradbury, not Bradley." This is always happening and irritates almost as much as the Doc business. But then I hate both names, so dull and uninspiring and somehow plain.

I reply that I'm a GP in Wormbridge. He repeats the name Wormbridge as though he hasn't heard of that either. I tell him I'm interested in Paul's post-mortem and how there was no cause of death.

"Isn't this unusual?" I ask him.

"Good God no!" he replies. He has a habit, when speaking, of belittling the person he is speaking to. I've met his type before and I don't let it put me off.

"So why did he die?" I say.

"No idea," he replies flippantly.

"Isn't that suspicious?" I say, "a young fit man

with no medical history being found dead in bed and a pathologists post-mortem finds nothing? Aren't the police involved?"

"Well, he didn't have a knife in his back, that might have been suspicious. You see, knife wounds, bullet holes, the police will be interested in those, not in this sort of rubbish."

I wasn't exactly sure what he was referring to as rubbish. Was it Paul, myself, Wormbridge?

"So what did he die of?" I persist.

"No idea," he says again, and this persistent and stupid response begins to annoy me.

"So, it's quite usual for a forty year old to drop dead when there is no reasonable cause of death?"

"Happens all the time."

"Right," I say. There is a sort of stonewalling going on here: professional killdeer perhaps. I've never played it with a pathologist before. Life does throw up some exciting opportunities.

Up until this point, still, the ejector seat is an option but what happens next means that now and for all the future I have fucked the ejector seat option, the slow descent can begin and there is no escape. But it's all so easy in retrospect isn't it?

So I say to him: "Did you have a close look at his feet?"

There was a pause and then he started again: "Who did you say you were?"

I repeated my name and I can hear him writing it down.

"So, Dr Bradley, are you accusing me of not doing my job properly?" There is a slight but perceptible shift in his voice, from the down right arrogant to the accusatory.

"Of course not, Dr Cape." I can play this Doctor naming game as well, and frankly I am pissed off with this arrogant bully of a man. "No it's just that I noticed there was an injection mark on his foot; faint but definitely present, and in addition I noted, when I was called to the scene of his death, that his shoelaces were done up in a different way. And it's Bradbury by the way."

He laughs a little which makes him sound like a teacher, a teacher and a bully. "So you're suggesting…" - he is speaking very slowly now, like I've got special educational needs and he wants to explain something to me - "…you're suggesting that some nasty person took off this man's shoe, injected him with a deadly-poison and then retied his shoe and let him die? Oh dear, oh dear. You've been reading too much fiction, Dr Bradley, or maybe it's the TV, I'm not sure which." At this point he suddenly changes his tone. "Are you not aware, Dr Bradley, from your clearly limited medical education that when humans die often small spots, called petechiae," he says this very slowly, "often appear on the skin and these can resemble injection sites?"

Oddly enough my 'limited medical education' has informed me of this fact, and this little provincial GP knows the difference between a petechia and an injection site. At the same time I realise I'm up against it here and in addition I have the first inkling of danger, of fear, that will later blossom like ugly weeds within me. So I do a sort of retreat and allow him to attack. I lead him, in this case, to the home of my incompetence and away from the fact that I think someone has killed Paul, for a motive that I am not aware of yet.

I allow him to continue: "So, you are suggesting that we leave the grave of this poor man empty and put the relatives through further torment because you can't tell the difference between a ruptured capillary and an injection site?'

"I'm sorry," I say, promptly, "I wasn't aware of that fact and I certainly wasn't questioning your professional capabilities. His poor girlfriend has been through the mill. It's just that I wanted to be sure. I was trying to do my job you understand, but you've answered my anxieties, so I must apologise."

He mumbles something that I don't hear and then he continues: "I suggest you concentrate on the sore throats and the earaches and leave the forensic pathology to the experts."

I avoid the bait although, bile (if that's medically possible), is filling my stomach. I thank him for his kind assistance and then put the phone down.

Afterwards I realise that I've been stupid. But then I'm always being stupid. As long as I learn from these mistakes then by the end of my career I will not be stupid anymore. Anyway, I am ready to drop this whole thing: I'm going nowhere, and there is just too much to do without trying to play the detective as well; being the priest and the shaman is exhausting enough.

So I throw the report into the filing tray. I am determined not to spend any more time on Paul or on any of this. I feel I've made the decision and I'm already looking forward to a wild night with the boys from Bristol tonight: a band, some beer, some smokes and lots of chat, lots of philosophy, drunken philosophy.

By the time I give the tray to Sheila though, I've had to reconsider my position. In my in tray there is now an application for life insurance from Julian.

Then I think of what Alan said, the man down on the Bristol Road at the car wreckers. What he says often comes back to me in odd ways. It's like I have almost all the components around this Paul business to make it work, but like the car there is one crucial thing that I haven't got, and once I have got the equivalent of that differential joint, then it will all hang together; it will start to roll. Up until this point there is just a myriad of separate components.

## CHAPTER EIGHT

As an exercise in collecting human stories, my job has no equal. I sit amongst the blue carpet, the computer, the couch in the left hand corner, the filing cabinet, a few leaflets, the big wide window that looks out over geraniums. People come and deposit their stories, like I'm a savings bank for them. I have in mind something out of Jorge Luis Borges, where every story that's ever been told, or can be told, is waiting, already reported, already chronicled in my notes. Awaiting some sort of filing, awaiting someone who will one-day root through and pick out some theme that illuminates the whole of mankind.

Sometimes it's just as if that's my only job: to listen to stories and document them, like some Kafkaesque clerk. So when I'm not working, I don't want to hear any stories at all. I want to get drunk and dance and talk, talk back and laugh and listen to music and do, just like Rosie says, what normal people do.

So tonight I go down to Bristol, without Rosie and see some of my friends. I feel the need for a good night out.

Claude lives in Bristol. Claude is French but he lives permanently in Bristol. He likes it here, or so he says. He used to be married to an Englishwoman, but he's not married any more, he lives in a typical bachelor pad: suavely designed, modern and lacking a chaotic soul such as a Frida Kahlo might bring to it. We talk about this a lot, and he once said that Frida Kahlo was his ideal woman: a bit wild, violently possessive, but filled with vibrant warmth. He says that she would put flowers all over the place and leave fruit scattered on the table.

Claude is an anglophile except when it comes to football, where he supports France. He is no fool and I've admitted many times that I would do the same, in his shoes.

We call him the Professor because he is wise, no matter what he's drunk or smoked, wise like he says things that you weren't even close to thinking and wise with small sensible pieces of wisdom. And can this man drink! That's one thing he has adopted from us Brits. He drinks pints like they are nothing.

Claude is not particularly good looking, his hair is good, mind and he's kept all of it, but his face isn't attractive. It has that odd capacity, once you've been with him for a few hours, of becoming more attractive, as though it is absorbing the richness of his character.

I'm staying with Claude; I always do.

Round to his house comes Marcus, who used to be married as well, but now has a much younger girlfriend, who used to be a student of his. Like I said he's proud of this although she - Claude and I have always thought - is a bit of an airhead. Trophy, we sometimes call her. She looks pretty spectacular and when you look pretty spectacular you can get away with saying some pretty stupid things. Marcus is an art teacher and an abstract artist on the side with a passion for old cars.

The three of us are the philosophers. Marcus, I think, would love to form some artists' group, like the fauves or the surrealists, so that he could talk the wanky artist talk with the two of us, but we steadfastly refuse to be taken down the abstract art theoretical trail. I admit that once I tried writing abstract poetry: I tried abstracting what it is that makes the feeling of words down to a basic non linear structure and then I completely gave up because, well, I have no wish to be the first abstract poet.

Beside the trophy issue and the occasional art issue, Marcus is great. He challenges me and I like that.

We start at the Arnofini, before heading out to St Paul's. The Star is packed and soon we are in a car with a friend of Marcus', heading for a party somewhere up in Clifton. A party in a tent, someone says. The tent itself is designed around a wild west motif, with swing doors and bar staff dressed as cowboys. Claude and I sit in one of the booths and watch Marcus flirting with some young women, who seems to be laughing both with him and at him.

Then everything gets twisted for a while and we dance like bears and drink more. The music is T Rex and old Will Smith and Jurassic Five and all sorts of other shit. I begin to swear too much, I see a woman taking a swing at Marcus. Later it transpires that she says he went for a grope. She is Bristol and not without her charms but her face is rugged where once it was beautiful. She wears a white dress that's tight to her skin. I'm never sure whether Marcus really would do such a thing, but he gets a kicking anyway. Claude is rolling by now and we dance like two married men would dance: trying not to attract attention, sexually neutral.

As the night goes on, though, so does an odd feeling that builds up. I am swaying and belligerent, but I begin to get this overwhelming feeling. This is when I know that all the Maria business is getting to me. I am in a Circus tent somewhere in Bristol, off my head, with my best friends and I feel unsure and I have this strong sensation that I am being watched.

Sometimes, when people go mad (properly mad), they experience feelings such as these. It is childish and introspective to think that people are watching you: why should anyone watch you? It's as bad as thinking that the TV is talking directly to you. I weigh this up in my drunken state. It's like a violin playing inside me, gradually getting higher and higher. I can work out what the sound is and then I can't. There is that terrible randomness when you're drunk. Claude seems fine, he carries on dancing and grinning his head off. Marcus is away with some other people now and the woman in the white dress is gnashing her teeth. When I first arrive, everyone in here seems so exotic, attractive. That's the problem with working in Wormbridge; almost anywhere is exotic and voluptuous when you spend most of your time in Wormbridge.

As the night goes on, I still can't quite relax. I drink more and dance with Claude and with some other people I vaguely know. Dancing should be obligatory for everyone each week. I'm really feeling quite unsteady and time is doing that thing of elongating again, and also compressing itself, as though it is an accordion being played. I feel the need to be stretched out and somehow cleansed myself. It's about at this moment that I notice him.

Now, although this evening I have recognised a slight paranoia, it's at this point that I realise that I've really lost it and, in addition, become far to enwrapped in my job. I am certain that I have just seen Paul, standing by the door which is modelled on the wild west and which are still swinging. Now, I do know that Paul is dead as I have certified him in a room in Queens Hill, and I also suppose that many people can look like Paul, he isn't that recognisable, so I run to the still swinging doors. The light outside is bright by the entrance but quickly turns to a darkness that is almost green, like a dark river, in its consistency. There are a few people talking who look around when I appear and then look back again. I am already feeling oh god, oh god, what is becoming of me. I physically shake my head to see if it will clear. I need to drink less.

Later I tell Claude about all of this. This is when

I'm back at his house and we're both smoking and drinking water and watching the light seep into the corner of his garden. I tell Claude everything. I told him once he should have been a doctor: he is a good listener, and he says he doesn't want to be a doctor.

He asks me why do I care. Why do I care about these people? How can I let them get to me? I tell him I frankly don't know. It becomes clear in my own head that, although I'm in the caring profession, I have never properly cared before and I can't put my finger on why I suddenly care about this Maria and another person who is dead anyway. Truthfully, I have no answer to his questions. I've always prided myself on the fact that my job has never got to me. In fact I feel, secretly, that doctors who can't handle the pressure are weak and rubbish.

Claude says that I must let it go. Seeing dead people, he reminds me, is a bit Hollywood and I need to get out more. We laugh. He is right. We effortlessly go on to talking about Marcus and what is going on with him. Claude decides that it's a mid-life thing albeit an early midlife thing. Marcus, in my opinion, has always been a little weak and in need of constant affirmation. In a stable relationship, there's just not enough affirmation. It's a hungry animal, that lust for affirmation. It consumes in the end. But Marcus is OK because by living the affirmation treadmill - as long as he never stops - there isn't enough time for thinking about yourself. It's a bit like pretending, all the time, to yourself: sort of pointless. What is it that he's hiding? What's he leading himself away from?

I only work the afternoon (thank god), that next day. My head is like drizzle. There is a toxic tinge to my guts. I think with dread that I've got Justin's fortieth to go to tonight at the Oak. I thought that perhaps a couple of nights out would sort me; reformat my head, but now the thought of dressing up as Madonna and talking to all sorts of people like Justin fills me with an even deeper nausea than I currently feel.

Just when I'm feeling like cruising through afternoon surgery, the first person I see, lounged over the desk in reception, is Julian. I think that I could whip round to the back door and avoid him if I'm quick but he's already seen me, so I have to smile and walk up to him.

"Ah Doc," he says, and I flinch inside, "They was saying you weren't here, and then you are here." He is with another man who I have never seen before. The other man is a bit older, early receding hair, in fact hair that seems to have three phlanges of hair pointing forward. He is expensively clothed and turned out, in a rather nouveau riche way but with no taste whatsoever, and is also just a little bit intimidating. I don't know why, but he has that look to him.

The receptionist is mouthing something that I don't get. Julian leans back on the desk like he is on a liner awaiting a cocktail. He is so full of arrogance he might well explode.

"Just a quick word, doc."

There is no way out of this, so I pick up my box

and lead him down the corridor. The older man tries to come with him but I indicate he needs to wait in the waiting room. He doesn't look very pleased. On the top of the box is a huge form I need to fill in about my new contract.

Julian chatters idly as we walk. I think for a moment that Julian and I are almost diametrically opposed: he is handsome, easy, cool, lazy and useless. At least I'm not lazy. Around his neck is a big silver cross that he wasn't wearing before.

"Is that a fashion thing or what?" I ask him.

"I'm not some sort of Goth, if that's what you're thinking," he says. "Just recently I've found the Lord, that's all. Is it funny or something?" He becomes vaguely threatening, but there are threats and threats and this man just doesn't scare me.

"No, no, it's not funny. That sort of thing is quite serious. No, it's just that you don't seem the type, that's all."

"What, you can't see the devil-dodger in me? Well funny you should say. I never saw it either."

"So, what's with the sudden change?"

He nods sagely, and I think a bit stupidly as well. "A friend showed me why it was important."

" What, your friend out there."

"What, Clive, no it wasn't him. But he's not a friend really, I just work with him."

"What sort of religion do you go in for then?"

"Just straight forward God stuff. It's not what you're thinking: it's not the Jehovah shit. It's no weirdo stuff. It's just straight Christian."

"Good," I say a bit distracted. I ask him what he wants to talk about. It turns out it's the insurance report, can I make it quick. They need it quick. I ask him why he needs it quick.

"It's work: they need me to be insured. They say they do this for all their staff after a while."

"I didn't think you worked," I say.

"I'm no slacker if that's what you mean. I do trips and stuff."

"Who for?" I ask.

"What's with the questions doc? It's just an insurance report.'

"I'm just curious," I say, although going through my mind is this idea that when I do finally sign his insurance form, it will be signing his death warrant. All of this, of course is unsubstantiated, so I could never be held responsible, but, nevertheless, I do feel responsible. Part of that Hippocratic oath that mythically doctors have to sign up to says I will do no harm. If I sign this report, I'm pretty sure, Julian will die. In terms of pattern recognition, it's an easy one to spot.

That's, after all, about the sum of what I do. Recognise patterns. OK, two things then, collect stories and recognise patterns and there's a rather strong one emerging here. There's something about business and southern Mexico and there's something about life insurance and suddenly dying. Is there something else I've missed? Well perhaps it's that they all involve me, I'm the doctor. Is it something about me? Is it me that part of the pattern is related to?

I tell Julian that I'll do it within a couple of days. His notes are wafer thin and it won't take more than ten minutes to go through that lot, but there are one

## Smallpox Hill

or two things I want to get straight in my head, including my head itself, and a few vague ideas that seem to crop up all the time at the moment.

"Who's paying for all this?" I ask him. I really don't believe it's his vicar.

"The people in charge," he says.

I wait and see whether anything else will be offered but he remains silent. "And who's in charge?' I ask. I'm a doctor and I can ask anything.

He looks evasive for a bit. I can see he's weighing it all up in that slacker brain of his.

"I can't really tell you that Doc," he says finally and then he languidly gets up and starts making preparations to leave. I notice his grace again and that he's got a set of new clothes; his Vans trainers are too white for the rest of him, too new so that they stand out.

I open the door wide and smile my benign doctors smile. I fill out his report and then, because its Friday afternoon, I sling it onto the side and leave it for Monday to check.

It's worked to a degree: the night out and talking to Claude. I feel different and less strained. I race through my surgery, finish early, drive home beneath Smallpox Hill with its line of trees, get home and briefly fall asleep. There is a note from Rosie. It says, 'Shall we go together?'

As I pick up the note, a man walks past the house, in the lane outside. I notice that he is dressed in these rich satin clothes, with gold braid and large obsequious brass buttons. He doesn't look in on me as such, but I can tell he's aware. His hair is shoulder length, greasy and seedy on top, but it's the way he walks I notice most particularly: it's like a sheep dog, sideways, a different direction than you would predict from his bodies position. He sidles as he walks, and then I become aware that he is actually limping and that his arm on one side is all bent up and useless. I wave to him, but he doesn't notice.

So Rosie wants to see me. That's something. Whether it's because she doesn't want to go to the party alone or because she wants to go with me remains to be seen. I fish out a few things I have in the bottom draw and then decide I'll walk up to Rosie's cottage. It's still hot although now the heat has changed to a heaviness, like a storm is about again. It turns the colours to more passionate shades, the humidity does, and creates within the valley a feeling of tropical intensity. The walk is good, like a meditation, and as I walk, I begin to look forward to the party and even more, to seeing Rosie.

It's best to follow the tree line that fringes the hills in our valley. Herdsley is set like an apple on a big plump cushion. It is ringed by low hills all around that some good person planted after the Second World War. Huge straight beech trees all silver and grey like elephant legs. There's a footpath just at the foot of these, just before the grazing line starts. Some of the beech has become elaborate as the soil is washed from their roots so that large chambers exist under their roots as though the landscape has been created by Gaudi and not God.

Rosie lives just about on this line, west facing,

just under the woods. I like to walk up here but today, although I feel more positive, something is bugging me. It must be some effect of the night out and Claude, but I feel like I'm not entirely alone. It is a difficult and complex feeling to discuss and I realise that chemicals are not good for me, not anymore, but I am unnerved. The last half a mile or so I just feel anxious. I'm getting to the stage I can't relax. Maybe I should take something. I hand out pills everyday and yet I don't really believe in any of them. And now I'm sounding like Rosie: you don't believe in yourself Nick, she will say, you're so cynical you've stopped believing. You see how stuff goes on inside me.

Rosie sees me coming and although it's not *Gone with the Wind* and she doesn't come running, I can feel a real excitement. Rosie is small, and she stretches up on toes and hangs her arms around my neck and we kiss for a long time. I'd forgotten about her mouth and the lovely taste she is. I'd forgotten her smell, her rich saltiness or the way her eyes close.

We don't say much and we go inside, out of the late afternoon blast of sun. Later we have a bath together and then we get dressed up, me as Madonna and her as Guy Ritchie. Rosie moans because Guy is so boring. I sometimes think that's why Madonna liked him in the first place. If you could have anyone in the world, you'd probably go for just an ordinary person, no one that's exceptional. That's until you get bored anyway.

I have on my blond wig and my leotard underneath, just in case. I look good as a girl: my shoulders are narrow and I've got a face that, for a man, is slightly long and daubed, but as a woman, it has elegance. The stockings and the short mini skirt are Rosie's and are tight but I squeeze in. She puts lipstick on my lips, carefully and mimics how I should rub my lips together. Then she brings the eye pencil and begins to draw on the soft eyelid skin, as though she is sketching, in short puckering pencil marks. There is so much silence up here, I hear only Rosie gently humming to herself and smell her newly washed body.

I'll take some time off with the new contract and go away with Rosie. The later light of the evening is more direct and cast a shadow across her vertebrae. I don't know what it is about Rosie, I can't say what exactly she does, but when I'm with her like this, I know she is exactly right for me. It is that mixture of security and something unobtainable within her: something that I can never have.

It seems a waste to go to a party this evening. The lights fill the sky above the pub before merging like phosphorus clouds with the twilight. The car park is scattered with men dressed as women and the sharp scattered smell of matches being lit.

Rosie doesn't like going out. She hates the small talk and the fickle falseness of it all. I, on the other hand, am an expert: making small talk is my absolute speciality. The party is heaving by the time we get there. I buy drinks and then a nurse I vaguely know starts talking to me and before I know it, Rosie's not there and I'm getting drunk again. I slap Justin on the back, like we are best buddies and he says something comradely into my ear about us sticking together through this age business, how the likes of him and me are the future of Wormbridge. He says this with his deep sonorous voice, like it's a speech or something. Soon he turns his back again and is touching some woman on the shoulder idly as he speaks to her.

After another couple of hours, sweat running down from under my wig and ruining my make-up and after a few men and women have pinched my bum, I think I'd better find Rosie and get home. There's always a feeling of depression at these parties: the same heavy breasted women getting drunk, the same men eyeing up the younger women, the older men touching their bald heads. I chatter on but I hate it all. I am false and baseless after all, and anyway there's so much killdeer in here that I could scream. So I go outside.

I'm really not sure afterwards whether I'm glad I go out at that time or whether it would have been better to have another beer and stare at more men dressed as Madonna. But I'm sort of glad that I find out. I think, afterwards, that I would have hated not knowing even more than I hate knowing. It's all so inglorious and ugly, so superficially tragic and on a deeper level, irrelevant and petty, a meaningless drama in our little sordid village.

So I step outside; the car park is almost empty. The lights are on, but it's that neon that although it pretends to be flooding the area with light, you can't actually see much detail in.

The door to Justin's car is open. There are two

people in there, one dressed as a woman and another as a man. The woman, dressed as Guy, has her neck pulled back and her legs hanging out of the door of the car, the open door. Her lips are pressed to a man's lips, who is wearing a blond wig. It's not accidental, that kiss, it lasts what feels like a lifetime. I stand there, transfixed to the spot, startled and ashamed. As I turn to walk away, Rosie somehow manages to break it off, and screams my name. I start running.

I mean she could have found somewhere a little less public than the car park at The Oak on Madonna night.

As I start running I have a stupid thought: how would Guy respond to something like this? Would he have run, like me, or come over all Jason Statham and challenged Justin Whatmore, knocking him out and then carrying Rosie home. Did Guy feel like this when he was chucked by Madonna. It's like I could cry and fight and lie down and go to sleep, all at once. I do none of these. I just keep running.

# CHAPTER NINE

I am not aware of this, but as I run down the long level road below Limcombe Golf Club, and past The Yeoman pub where its chucking out time and its all getting heavy, I've still got my blond wig on, mascara, miniskirt and, worst of all if anyone gets that far, a tight black leotard underneath, Rosie's leotard.

I don't know how I'm going to get home. I walk past Maria's house and look to the upstairs window where Paul was found dead. I think of going to see Maria and maybe borrowing some clothes and scrubbing my face, but the last time I saw her, she was screaming like I'd just eaten her children. Also she's a patient, and I, after all, am a doctor.

So I carry on running, with no hope of a lift, the blond wig askew and fighting back two urges: one is to cry, the other is to hit someone, preferably Justin Whatmore.

Rosie picks me up, in the end. She doesn't say

anything; I don't say anything. She leaves me at my gate.

That next Monday, I am feeling a lot better: Life can throw up some strange paradoxes, and, lets face it, the night at the Oak at Justin Whatmore's fortieth birthday was not a roaring success, and yet I feel better in a peculiar way. At least it's quite clear what's happening to Rosie and me. That was one of the things I had brooded over. I can now be categorical and say there is a major problem with Rosie, who was my girlfriend, and probably isn't anymore.

There is a sense that the world is beginning again. I recognise this state as shallow insubstantial optimism that can't help but go, but even so, I am enjoying the uncluttered feel it gives me.

I get in to work early and whip through the new contract forms, pages and pages of them. Next I turn my attention to Julian's insurance report. Just before surgery starts, I ring the number at the top of the form and very efficiently get answered. A woman listens to my query. Before she gives out details of who is paying for the report on Julian, she just needs to check. However it's not her who comes back on the line, but a man, who sounds like he means business and isn't averse to a bit of straight talking. He asks me who I am, and I repeat my name, my address, but then he cuts me off. He cannot divulge who is paying for the insurance report, but he guarantees that I will be paid in full.

I ask him whether they are regular clients and he answers yes. Where is their head office? At this, he delays and some music comes on. It's Rod Stewart's *Maggie May*, and like all good heartbreaks, every bloody minute of the day seems to remind me of Rosie and how I wished I'd never seen her face. How selfish we become with love; the world is just there to remind you of what you have lost.

Another man comes back, and the attitude is different: Why do I want to know all this? I tell him I'm just a GP and need to be sure that I get paid for this. He tells me that they always pay their bills; there is no need to worry. I try delaying for a bit but he isn't about to spill any particularly interesting beans. Then he puts the phone down.

I'm not getting particularly far here. There is one other thing I need to check. I ask the receptionist for the man's records who lived upstairs at Maria's before Paul: the junky with the worst complexion in Wormbridge, who had died of an overdose.

Ten minutes later, after the first patient, they tell me they have sent them back to the health authority. So I tell them to ask for the records back.

Morning surgery is filled with minor revelations and small crises. There is a litany at work in Wormbridge: a shallow feeling of depression and lack of hope. That I've chosen to settle here sometimes surprises me: it could have been Jamaica, or St Kitts or West Wales and I've gone for the Cotswolds for, in terms of decision making, basically reasons of pure chance. I would never have guessed.

They phone me when the last patient has left. The health authority has lost the notes. They've looked high and low and they can't find them. Well it's lucky that some relative isn't trying to sue me.

How can something like that get lost?

Everything I do is thwarted. Claude told me to give up, but if I give this up I really won't have anything going on at all. And there's something not right here either. It's not common that they lose some patients' records; they would be hauled through the courts if any one got to hear of this.

I carry on my day as thoughtlessly as possible. What I'm really dreading is after work, not the work itself. When the big hole left by Rosie will suddenly become apparent.

I notice that Maria is booked to see me this afternoon. It's the first time I've seen her since the funeral and since her screaming hatred. I'm looking forward to seeing her, I realise. I don't know what you would call it but there is certainly something exciting about her coming in. I suppose I just feel a little too complicit in her life.

I talk to Sue briefly, but she never has any time, well none for me anyway. I've always thought Sue has a hard joyless outlook on life. She is one of those who seem to take the challenge of surviving life a little too seriously and therefore leaves no room for actually enjoying it.

I buckle down to a bit of no-nonsense paper work; finish off the new contract. I'm applying for virtually exactly the same, having said all those proud words. I am all talk.

Then I have a blinding flash of inspiration. Now I don't get many of these and it gives me a healthy zap of excitement. All letters and reports that come to the surgery are scanned. We will have a record somewhere of the post mortem of the junky, that, and hopefully, some other things.

I persuade my computer to go into his records and sure enough, sitting there, is a full post mortem report. As usual it makes dull reading. The body was old and no toxicology is therefore available but the cause of death is postulated as accidental and due to an overdose of Diamorphine. However none of this interests me, it's just the name I'm after; sure enough, it's there, Pathologist reporting, one Dr Cape.

I check back and find no evidence of anything apart from a sad little poem surrounding prescriptions for methadone and failed urine tests and more failed tests and more words of consternation. There is one entry, by Sue, saying form done. That's it. Form done, it could have been any form. A referral form, a blood form. And it could have been an insurance form. But I am doubting myself again. Am I seeing and reading too much into this, creating evidence because I want it to be there. He was just a junky, after all, and probably Dr Cape was about right. The only question was why Dr Cape had done the PM at all. That is what perturbs me. Again though, I'm no further on.

The window of the surgery looks right over to Queens Long Down: a spine of a hill that seems, from the Escarpment, as though it's a huge boned whale washed up onto the shores of the Severn Estuary. Sometimes it feels as though the landscape itself is the only thing that keeps me together. I look and I long to be up there blown about by the warm wet westerlies or the fierce cold easterlies that come in January and February. But I'm not up there, I am in here; waiting for the next instalment of my life to start, or, more particularly, my evening surgery.

Maria is about third in. As she walks towards me initially I think she's back to normal: all sighs, head down, eyes nearly closed; the shrugged indifference. As she nears my desk, though, she looks up, straight at me, and holds my gaze with her fierce clear green eyes. She doesn't mention the last time we met, she sort of grunts at me instead and shifts her head back a little. It is clear that Maria is all there; she isn't too doped up and she's looked after her face. Her skin itself isn't in pristine condition but it's clear and axelottle, as though, like the insect, you might be able to see through to her deeper organs; a fragile surface. She doesn't look down, she just stares at me.

"You get the report?" she says at last.

I nod. It's painful but important that Maria makes the running here. The silence is begging to be filled with words and swirls around us, the uncomfortable creature that silence is.

"How can you die of nothing?" she continues, "haven't you got to die of something?"

"I rang up. Apparently it's quite common."

Again there is silence. I can feel Maria's presence almost more than I can see her. She exudes this confusing scent of chaos, longing, regret and above all damage. But beyond that, like a top note, there is this animal thing I can't put my finger on: this will, this indomitable strength.

I never really get to where Maria is. She is

beyond my realm of reference.

"Have you been cutting?" I ask her.

She says nothing but she pulls up her sleeves and her arms look remarkably good for her. There is all the old scarring that distorts the flow of skin: the pale useless scar tissue where the wounds have broken down, the crisscrossing like some latticed tart, but nothing new.

I don't understand Maria and I don't get her cutting either. Why isn't she cutting now? In my simplistic way, I would have put good money that she would be cutting just about any parcel of skin she could get her hands on, after what she's been through. Yet she is clean and moreover, calm.

"Nice funeral?" I say.

"What," she says. "How can it be nice?" She pauses for a bit and the silence is dangling horribly.

"Why did you scream at me so, that last time?" I ask, so as to break that blankness.

She doesn't smile but she nods. She is serious today.

"I hated you touching him, that was all. He was mine and I didn't want any twat touching him. I had enough of that with that wanker from the undertakers."

I usually pull Maria up on her language. This time, however, I couldn't have put it better myself. I feel like I'm warming up. Maria always has this effect on me. I suppose it's why I've wasted so much of my time trying to help her.

There is another long silence and Maria pushes her slightly greasy blond hair back. Then she asks why I was checking Paul's feet.

She's refreshingly clear of playing games today, it's up to me whether I want to deceive her, but the more I think of it the more pointless I realise it would be. The only real reason I'm so mixed up in this is because I'm worried about Maria: I feel she is sort of vulnerable. I realise I care about her, which is lucky because I'm in the caring profession. So I make the decision that there's no point in being careful and lead her away from where my concerns lie.

"I don't know about Paul, I might be acting crazy but sometimes I wonder whether someone, well, helped him die. I don't know, killed him."

Her reaction to this removes all my doubts: she doesn't react; it is not news to her, she just looks long and hard at me, like a voyeur might. I feel the full hotness of her look, as though her eyes themselves could give off a heat. I'm really not sure what I'm doing now. I hadn't thought that this might all come up, that we would be brought to this, and now I'm not sure what to do next. So I do nothing but stare back into her eyes and her face. I could stay like this for hours, but then she starts.

"Why look at his feet?"

I explain the shoelaces and the tiny spot that looked like an injection site. Then I tell her about the radio and that, if she is right and Paul always hated the radio, there must have been someone in that room who turned on the radio after he was dead. Next I tell her about Dr Cape and his not exactly friendly reception and then I stop, because, well, that's about it, apart from a few insurance reports. In the silence that follows I realise what I have is a pretty ropey set of clues.

After I've petered out the silence comes back, like a mist returning as the sun grows weaker. She, I think, is weighing things up, wondering what should happen next.

There is something in the medical textbooks about when people look up above your head and (I think) to the right. This means, apparently that they are about to tell you something important. Or is to the left, I can't really remember. I always think of it as staring at the horizon and thinking madly. Anyway, Maria is looking above my head and slightly to the right and her green eyes are wide and made with glass. So I wait, and this time I don't blow it by talking.

Finally she starts talking again, "Don't get involved in this shit." All that thinking time and she comes up with this.

"What shit?" I ask her.

She says, "Oh," and waves her hand like it's all too much, which in a sense, it is.

There's a very long pause now.

In the end I start again, slowly, "So, what happens is someone is killing people and then collecting their life assurance, somehow. Is that right?"

She sort of 'pahs' me, like French people do, as though they're almost laughing at you but also making you aware that you're way off: you don't get it.

"The life insurance is nothing. Nothing.'

"So why did they kill Paul then?"

The words Paul and kill together are, I agree, a

little harsh and she blanches. But in reality, this is what we are talking about.

"Look, I told you not to get involved. You don't want them to turn their attention to you, do you? You've already made a bit of a name for yourself. Just drop it. It doesn't matter to you."

"Paul was one of my patients and he got killed. Another of my patients is about to die as well, and Maria, it will be you soon, that's what I hate." Maybe the hate bit sounds wrong, but there, I've said it.

She smiles this little smile that, in terms of facial expressions, she's only just invented. It's a new one, suggesting very slightly that she has more of a handle on this than I imagine she has. But I'm never sure about Maria. And I'm getting even less sure, if that's possible.

"The life insurance is just an after thought, a nice little earner." She looks down at her feet again. This is a more normal position for Maria, eyelids covering eyes, head hung forward like she's either thinking deeply or just giving up.

"The main business is keeping people quiet. For ever."

There is a long pause.

"Funny thing is, they didn't know we got married. They don't know everything, not everything."

I look at her incredulous. "What, you got married before he was killed?"

"Is there something wrong with that?"

A sudden thought hits me, like a wall of wind coming up from the sea: knocks me clean off my killdeer feet. Is Maria involved in this? And if she is, what exactly is she involved in?

"Maria, look, I've got to like you. I mean…" I tail off because, having started, I'm not sure how I'm going to say this. Not sure really where it's going and for that matter, where I'm going.

"I mean, are you in on this? Are you making money? Are you working for them, the people doing the killing?"

'What are you saying? Me working for The Brothers? What have you got for brains, shit or something!'

I take the insult because, I suppose, I deserve it.

"Who are The Brothers, Maria? Are they the ones doing the killing?"

She stops now because I suppose she realises she's said too much, or at least it's getting complicated. My mind is spinning. I believe Maria when she speaks. I really don't believe she is involved with killing people. She's just damaged and I've got this fairly heavy inkling that her damage and Paul's murder are linked.

She changes tack very suddenly. "My uncle died," she says, looking out the window at the electric purple geraniums and the picture of Rosie that I've tipped over for the day so that she's face down on my window sill and, more importantly, I can't see her face.

"Remember I told you about him? Stanley who owned the pub. He was good to me, he was. He hated The Brothers, but for some reason they left him alone." It's like she's talking to someone else, or at least for someone else's benefit. I've lost her somewhere. I've lost her to another round of killdeer.

"Midge was there, at the end. She said it was a happy death, well, if death can be happy."

Maria peters out because, in truth, her heart wasn't into talking about her uncle. She is just doing it to keep words coming from her and to keep the prying silence away.

"Funny really, his lease ran out about a week before he died. Midge said he sort of hung on until the lease was finished, and then let himself go."

Then, unexpectedly, Maria starts crying. Now, I've known Maria for years, through her ups and rather more frequent downs and yet I realise that I've never seen her cry. When we cry we take on a whole new character, because crying is a biological thing, so that the character of our crying is independent of what we would like it to be. Maria cries ugly, with lips all splayed and this odd equine sound. It is raw and untainted by civilisation. Loud as well, loud and coarse.

I have plenty of people crying in my room. There is a pattern in human behaviour that after a difficult disclosure, of which there are plenty in this room, there are often tears afterwards. The tissues are always close by and I become adept at whisking a couple out and almost mindlessly giving them to people. I usually feel it's some sort of success when people cry in my room: I feel I have brought on a catharsis of sorts. This time it feels sort of helpless, like we've been pretending for ten minutes that everything is fine and it suddenly becomes apparent that everything is not fine at all, it's all so fucked up, this world, and she and I are surrounded by its sadness.

So I grab her hand and hold it in mine. It's something I often do; it's not especially for Maria. It's probably a bit crass but it feels the right thing to do.

And then, equally unexpectedly, I start to cry as well.

Now, I realise that doctors are not meant to cry and luckily I am the silent crying type, so no one but Maria will ever know. It must be all this tension, all the Rosie business and oh, I don't know really why I'm crying, but I am and so is Maria.

I take some more tissues for myself and after a few minutes we have both stopped and although my breathings a bit out of kilter, I feel much, much better, like someone has untwisted me.

"So these Brothers, what can we do about the Brothers?"

"Best thing, like I said, is to not get involved."

"The Brothers is what, then? Are they like some sort of mafia, a family thing?"

She just nods. And then she shakes her head and looks down. "They're called The Brothers still but there's only one left now."

"It's not that friend of your ex –stepfather?"

"What Clive, that stupid little shit! Of course not. He would love to be one of the Brothers. He just does a bit of their dirty work. Anyway, you've met him already. In the surgery, Remember?"

I pause for a moment

"What's this dirty work, apart from killing people?"

She stops and makes an odd shape with her mouth. "You don't want to know. They make money, lots of money. They like to think they help out the poor. You don't want to know any more, I promise you."

"Maria, that's where you're wrong. I *do* want to know."

"It can only end one way if you get involved. So just don't. It ain't going to help anyone even if you do."

"It might help *you*."

"Who do you think you really are? Do you really think you can stop what's going on? You'll just disappear. That was what used to happen, before they fell onto the life assurance stuff." She comes to a stop, like her voice is left in midair. Then she wipes her eyes, slightly angrily, like she is cross with them.

"Just start being a doctor again."

I start to speak, but she interrupts me. "I've known these people all my life. They come over all holy and then they just do what the fuck they want. Just forget it all."

I nod finally, because I'm going nowhere. I can see she is getting bored of this and I let it go.

She stands up finally. I don't know what to say now. It's as though we've both given up our innermost secrets to each other and now it's a bit embarrassing and we don't know where to put our hands. Then I put my hands on her notes: they are huge, like as big as an *Unsuitable Boy* or the *Bible* in large print: a great big epic.

"That's one thing," I say to her, "you'll never get

life insurance for yourself in a million years."

We both laugh. It's a good moment. I realise that she's been under this pressure her whole life and I suddenly see a lot of things about Maria. She hasn't really told me much today but I know I'm closer to her now: closer to her hidden parts, her treasure.

At the end of surgery I walk back to reception. In the waiting room is Louise. I haven't seen Louise for a couple of years. She's a few years younger than me and her face, unexpectedly set in front of me, seems lithe, full of something, touchable and rather attractive.

She says something that makes me laugh. It feels immediately so effortless. We used to have something, Louise and I, but we were both so casual it just sort of got lost.

I invite her out, the next day. We arrange a time quickly. Then I remember that I must phone my Mum, I haven't phoned her since this all began. She's all alone these last two years since Dad died. I am a crap son. So I phone and we gossip for an hour and a half and gradually I hear her cheering up. Being an only child is a heavy responsibility and one which I am not really up to.

On the way home, I see the man dressed in his dark red and crimson uniform. He shuffles as he walks, past Cats Castle and by the side of Smallpox.

I must speak to him sometime.

# CHAPTER TEN

Summer erupts today, a great flowering of heat and everywhere is soaked in blue. In the Herdsley valley almost everything has burst open. Flowers are sated and hung heavy with seeds. On the radio they talk about a Spanish Plume, hot air rising in a bubble from the Iberian peninsular. I imagine it like a mushroom cloud pushing north and cloaking us in a lovely foreign heat.

I can hear Rosie on a morning like this, out in her dress and Wellingtons watering madly until the sun gets too hot and it makes it all pointless. It's the first morning I really miss her.

I walk down to the shops and buy bread and a bottle of wine. The village is bathed in a luminous stone like colour. The older people sit outside the post office and drink coffee from stainless steel tables that reflect the sun in odd shapes onto the newspaper stand.

# Smallpox Hill

I have a day off today. I think about Maria a bit and what these Brothers are, what they do, but I don't feel wound up in it. Not so much. I think of my contract, coming up for renewal, and Sue and my house and me and my mother.

I'm meeting Louise at noon, and we're going swimming in the river, in these deep pools that I know. It's just that, I suppose, I wish it were Rosie I was going with. Rosie always finds thing when we go off together. She has sharp eyes and an inquisitive mind and I miss them.

Sometimes it becomes clear that I really don't know what I want out of life. If only I did it would be so much easier.

Louise is great, though. She's straightforward and never plays games.

We walk down a path next to the river, for two or three miles. The river Avon trickles like the lazy green thing that it is. The sky is almost unbearably blue and there is a wind, a wind that is white and hot and Spanish.

Louise wears a loose white top and a tied up sarong from one of her fairly frequent trips to Thailand, and slender flip-flops. She has dyed blond hair held up loosely behind her head.

We scatter conversation about us like dandelion seeds. I tell her all about Rosie and how it feels to be dressed up as Madonna. She tells me about her series of nothing relationships with unworthy men. She knows Rosie vaguely. Everyone in Wormbridge knows everyone else. As I speak, although I feel unfaithful, it also feels like a release. Louise, for her part, seems to enjoy the unfettered details. How is it that people like you more when you show your weaknesses, when you show them you are an abject failure? She laughs loudly when I tell her about wearing the black leotard underneath and she tells me she'd like to see me in a black Leotard and I raise my eyebrows.

Maybe it's the wind and the heat together but today I feel a little crazy, like children get when it's really blowing, almost wild and above all carefree. We stop by the old mill all ruined and taken over with Ash trees, fallen beams and would-be fireplaces.

I realise I like being with Louise. She brings out a sort of reckless excitement in me. Whether it would last forever, I'm really not sure. I like the fact that neither of us cares whether it will last forever or not. Louise seems to me to exist solely in the present. There is no baggage and no issues around the future.

We find a place surrounded by walls made of brambles. The wind makes a racket and the river murmurs and moans in its sleep. We are in amongst the brambles and some old rotten tree trunks.

Louise takes off her sarong and lays it down on the green grass. The grass is soft, nibbled by rabbits, almost perfect like a golf course. I stretch out next to her.

Water flows through the broken wood of the weir, as though the river wants to show its sleek silver, fish like belly. The low hills around us, ground out by the river, are necklaced in haze and pollen. There is this feeling, on the hottest of days, that the summer will go on forever which is, of course, impossible. Even the grass seems to be screaming with delight.

I look down, my head is on my hand, I am lying on my side, looking down at Louise's face. There are faint blue lines around her eyes of old make-up and the deep shadow and who knows, maybe a few late nights.

I then lie on my back facing the sun and now she leans over me. I have that lovely feeling of sun on my skin and Louise tracing lines on my chest

I go swimming partly to cool off and partly to try and think straight. Is this the right thing to be doing? If, given my circumstances, I could choose, which I should be able to but can't seem to, would I be doing this? I put my hot head under the water and the cold river folds itself over my scalp.

All questions seem pointless, the weak man that I am, as when I return to Louise, she has taken her white shirt off.

She rests her head on my shoulder. I look down at her and she look up at me. I realise I don't really care what is wrong or right any more. So I kiss her and kiss her.

Afterwards we swim, like we are amphibians, which we are, partly; swim in the deep green river, wash down our bodies.

On the way back, instead of feeling scorched by the sun, I feel bleached by it. As though all the colours have been taken out of me.

I like that feeling.

We spend the evening and the night together in my house. She can drink, can Louise, and we sit out looking at the valley, chatting and smoking until the moon is high up and gives the trees that fringe Herdsley a silvery sheen. Louise has this effect of stopping me thinking.

I unplug the phone: I want to be outside of everything tonight. There's a sort of flow to Louise and me, a thread that we effortlessly pick up, whenever we meet. Sometimes it seems too easy to be with her, if that's possible.

I am woken at about 7 o'clock the next morning. I don't know why I wake so early. I plug the phone back in and it immediately starts ringing. I wake up feeling like ten gallons of the cheapest red wine has secretly been poured down my throat as I've slept. I think vaguely about work and patients and how somehow I will have to work all day. It's again hot outside, like its forgotten how to be anything else.

The phone is incessant and, in addition I can't find it. It's one of those cordless ones that allows you to pace as you talk. Finally I locate it, beneath a pillow on the sofa. It's Rosie.

Rosie always gets up early. The only difference is that she sounds, well, wrong today. I ask her how she is. Then she starts crying.

"My house has burnt down, Nick, I've lost everything, everything."

"Where are you, Rosie? Where are you now?"

She is still crying but she tells me she's at her

house. I ask her if she's alright and she says that she isn't hurt but the house is just…. But then she peters out. I tell her I'm coming over straight away. I put the phone down.

God… God. Why this morning? The house is upside down and Louise is sleeping in my bed, her clothes are everywhere, there are wine bottles and left out food.

I wake her. She can barely open her eyes. I tell her what has happened and she makes a slightly wry comment about Rosie and me and her, which doesn't sound particularly nice.

I say I'm sorry and kiss her a long time and tell her how good she is and what she's done for me. Then I run her home and go straight up to Rosie's house.

I can see the smoke from maybe a mile away, eddying up into the clear pristine sky. It has a sinister look, does smoke on a clear sky. Something malignant.

Rosie is pale and exhausted but unharmed. I hug her. I feel self-conscious that I might have the smell of Louise on me, and it crosses my mind just to tell Rosie, since anyway she was the one who started this. But when I look at her, there is an overwhelming feeling of pity and something like love, except that I don't really know what love is. I just can't tell her, not now when her house is smouldering with all her possessions smouldering as well.

I tell her that thank god she is alright and she bursts into tears again.

There are smuts on her face and her hair is all blown and wild.

I take her home and tell her how much I've missed her, which is only partly true. I put her in a deep warm bath with some nice oils in it, and as she soaks, I race around the house tidying, rip off the bed sheets and put some clean ones on. I feel like a nasty little prick and, in some ways, I am.

I ask her about the fire and she says the fireman reckon it was started in the hall near the front door. They couldn't decide what had caused it but said it was usually an electrical thing.

I bring her a cup of tea and toast, pop her into bed and then have to rush to work for morning surgery.

It's so busy, because I had the day off, that I really don't have time to think all morning. By midday, there is a message from Rosie saying could I ring before visits.

I feel I'm operating at about 100 miles per hour and I'm going to make a huge cock up, of probably everything, by the end of the day. I'm tired and the headache has got so bad that I've resorted to medium strength painkillers.

Rosie tells me that the police want to see her. I ask her why. At first she says something about insurance and then she begins to cry again. The police are pretty sure that the fire was started deliberately.

For the second time today I say God, about ten times in a row, and then a few stronger words as well. What exactly is happening here?

Now I know this can all be due to some random act of violence. Rosie's house is out on the edge of nowhere and no body will ever get caught getting away from there. But Rosie's not one of these people that would make enemies and the randomness just doesn't fit. In fact there's only one person that makes enemies around here and that's me. That's what makes me shiver, physically shiver. Is this something that is directed at me? But then, I get all rational and become the scientist that I am. They might be able to find out where I live, but not Rosie. Thinking this is about me is just paranoid. It probably isn't even an arson attack. Rosie's house was old and rickety and the wiring was ancient. It'll just be the police - probably that young, up his arse officer that I met before - getting all over excited.

So I try and relax and get rid of this toxic feeling that's located somewhere in my guts but seems to be emanating around my body like some chemical.

I get back home and give Rosie a lift to the police station. She is in there about two hours; I go back to the surgery and try and clear some of the backlog from the morning. I notice there is a message to ring Maria, but I haven't got time. I'll do it later.

Then there is a call from the station and this time the receptionist puts it through. The officer, instead of saying what I expected which is could you pick up Rosie, we've finished with her, instead asks me to report at the station within the next hour or so for questioning.

Me, they want to question me!

I haven't really got time for this. Sometimes it's

as though there isn't physically enough time to do this job, but maybe that's just me.

At the police station, Rosie is nowhere to be seen. A female officer who I haven't seen before mentions that she's been taken to stay with her mother. It seems odd that Rosie hasn't phoned to tell me, but I'm in such a rush that I don't give it much thought until later when it is pretty obvious.

By some ill-gotten chance, it's the young twat of an officer who gets the lucky chance of interviewing me. He takes me into a bare room with a table and a couple of chairs and sits me down. Right from the start, it's clear that his loathing of me will form the basis of the interview. Some cops just love the power of the job, the uniform, the radio, the ability to do what they want with you. This man loves that. I've met him a few times, before Paul's death and always it's the same. He despises me. You can tell by his lips.

He presents the case as such. I have just split with Rosie, having just caught her with another man in a car park at a party, 'carrying on' as the young cop puts it with some suppressed glee.

"You," that's me, "become bitter and to get back at her, as the jilted lover," the cop takes some time describing my perceived role, "the jilted, the rejected, the spurned lover."

How can anyone say that words are not the cruellest of all weapons?

So then I - according to the fired up young piglet in front of me - get cross and burn down her house.

I tell him that's ridiculous. I have never done

anything wrong or aggressive in all my life. I tell him how many times I've been cast off as a lover, which I think he enjoys, and how I've never done anything like this. The cop nods but then adds that Rosie has noticed that I've been acting very strangely of late. I, rather stupidly, laugh at him. That doesn't make me an arsonist, I tell him.

"So who was it?" he continues. "Your ex-girlfriend," he particularly enjoys saying ex, "can't think of any one else who has any sort of grudge against her, and meeting her, I believe her."

He leans back when he finishes speaking.

I, meantime, am frantically weighing up a few things in my head. I could put this one to bed, so to speak by just mentioning Louise, but then Rosie would know about her and me and I'm not sure if I want that to happen. And anyway, this jacked-up police officer is rather ahead of himself since they aren't even definitely sure this is arson or not. So I decide to hold fire on the alibi, until I have to use it.

I wonder why I'm so against Rosie knowing what I've been up to, but this is a personal thing. I know Rosie will hate it and I suppose, in the back of my mind, I would like Rosie back. At the base of all this is that I do love Rosie after all.

I think.

Anyway, I don't tell him about Louise. Instead I tell him I've got afternoon surgery and he tells me that although I can go, I'm a suspect and that there's plenty of evidence against me on this one.

I am mean all the way through evening surgery. I'm fast and mean and really shouldn't be allowed to be a doctor this afternoon. There is not an ounce of caring in me. I'm drifting all over the place and firing off randomly, as though I am that mad molecule that has had all the constraints taken away.

Also I'm exhausted. I regret having spent so much time with Louise and how much more complicated it has made my life. I regret not washing my hands of Maria, of The Brothers; I regret being cold and not marrying Rosie, once and for all.

I know that it doesn't help to live your life in regret but then I'm tired and most of all I'm all over the place.

So, it's been a bad day. The only trouble with a bad day is that it can, by the rules of chance, get worse just as much as it can get better.

I phone Maria, who usually just needs some extra medication, which I will give her as much as she wants today. Except, now she doesn't want medication. She needs to talk to me urgently, but can we meet somewhere other than the surgery or her house. God, I say again, and although I do not believe, I half feel that maybe I should try it, just like Julian. It might just help, at least, to have some sort of belief.

So I arrange to meet Maria the following morning, on one of the back roads out of Herdsley. On the way out of the surgery I see the man dressed in crimson velvet with the buttons and the limp. He walks up to me for the first time and says that I'm in a lot of trouble. I grab him and demand to know what he knows. How does he know I'm in trouble? Who told him? He does this irritating thing of staying silent. His face is slightly eschew, as though the threads that have formed it were pulled too tight on one side. How do you know? He tells me he can't say. This is when I do the only action that day that I regret. I scream what does he know and whom does he work for. I'm convinced that this man has been following me and finding out about Rosie's house, that he's somehow linked to all that has happened. He just smiles up at me, slightly crooked so it comes as a sneer, virtually.

"I've just been watching you," he goes on, "I've always been watching you." He does the smile again, and, it's been a bad day but this is no excuse.

I hit him in the face.

When I get home the phone is ringing again. I never quite get away; never have a proper haven up above the world where I can get my head together. It'll be Rosie, who I'd like to speak to, or Louise, who I would quite like to speak to, or Claude who I would really like to speak to or perhaps my Mum who I should speak to.

But it's none of these. This is the moment that, although the young cop and the arson charge and the new contract, and the loss of Rosie and the kind of unfaithfulness of Louise all seem a bit of a mess, they're nothing compared to what is about to happen. This is the moment when I realise properly that I'm out of my depth, that, in metaphor terms and colour terms, I'm sinking; the ocean is wide and it's all blue, everywhere without hope of another colour.

There is a man on the other end of the line, Local accent. He identifies himself as Clive, the friend of the ex-stepfather of Maria. He tells me, very slowly, without a hint of anger, that amongst other things I'm in trouble.

"The fire," he says, "is just the start. If you keep messing with The Brothers, if you keep questioning pathology reports and spreading malicious gossip about the place, such as insurance companies and company employees who have requested straight forward life insurance, then next it will be you; next it will be you that gets a little injection in the foot."

I ask him, "Are you threatening me?"

He coldly answers, "Yes."

Then, as an after thought, he says that there was no point trying to help Maria. She was just a screwed up little girl and if she made any more trouble…

"Oh and don't bother going to the Police again. They won't help either."

I tell him OK, OK and then the phone call ends.

I don't sleep. Not one wink. I smoke and smoke and drink but the sleep will not come.

# CHAPTER ELEVEN

If it carries on this hot, we will all self-combust and then there'll be nothing left to make me worry.

The news is all filled with talk of global warming and heat waves. People who do not usually wear sandals are wearing sandals. Just like when it snows, the heat brings on a festival type atmosphere to England, as though almost everything shuts down, or operates on the most skeletal of services.

The wind has gone. After the sunrise I manage to get a few hours sleep and now it's time to get shaved. I look carefully in the mirror and see the damage that time has dealt to my face; time and yesterday's sun. I make several expressions to it, goad it, and then feel slightly sick. Like I am an alcoholic in need of my first little eye opener. Or like the Consul Geoffrey Firmin in Under the Volcano.

There is an ache, like nausea, beginning to settle

in my stomach almost permanently. I shave carefully and then douse my head and body in the shower. If I can just get through today, then I think I'm going to be OK. All the worry will gradually lift. I'll start getting successful again; get back to what I was before.

There's only one problem. That is, I was beginning to hate my life, that's probably the reason I got so interested in Maria, got so mixed up and messed up. But at least I had some sort of control, some stance, some position, before all this. Now all I have is a great big mess and people telling me they're going to give me a lethal injection. Was there anything much to go back to, though, except a slightly heartless man who is going nowhere; who tries to avoid caring too much.

There's not much caring during morning surgery. Patients will be deserting me in their droves if I carry on like this. Or maybe they'll like the new streamlined Dr Bradbury more. Perhaps that's how they like their doctors. Hard and driven and straight. It always surprises me the somersaults and twists and turns that your mind will do to make you feel you're not as bad as you actually are.

I stagger to the end of it and ask Sue if she'll mind doing the two visits to patient's houses. She asks why and I say I'm having a hard time of things. I mention Rosie's house and she comes back fast like some Staffordshire Bull Terrier who never lets go.

"I heard you and Rosie were over. In fact I heard the police suspect you lit the fire."

I am ready to explode. All the shit I've taken off this woman's plate professionally, all the tricky drug addicts and personality disorders that I've looked after while she does the easy stuff, and now she appears in league with the young, up his arse officer, accusing me of this.

I've had just about enough and I intend to tell the police today about Louise and how we were together from noon the day before to the next day. It was stupid, I realise, to try and protect her, and Rosie. Lies and omissions tend to fester and divide, like bacteria multiply into huge growths, or pustules. Maybe I should tell the police about these murders too, except most of them are dead and buried and all the possible legalities and technicalities are covered. So I smile pleasantly at Sue and in the end she does the visits. The only difference is that now I hate her, hate her passionately, and she probably feels the same about me.

Now I feel like I've cleared the table, ready to tackle Maria, and whatever it is she wants to tell me. It's important, as a man, to do one thing at a time. Otherwise it can all get confusing.

She is, just like she said she would be, on the back lane out of Herdsley, next to the Pet Hotel where the dogs get given sofas and TVs to make their stay as comfortable as possible. She looks clean and undrugged. Together, in a Maria-ish sort of way. Her eyes are properly opened, but on top of this she is nervous. She has been smoking lots, I can tell by her fingers and she's smoking when I arrive.

She looks up and down the lane, like she is

wanting to dump something illegal. Then she jumps over the gate, more athletic than I give her credit for.

In many ways, it's remarkable what's happened to Maria over the last eight weeks. It's as though, after Paul, she has galvanised herself. Where before events happened to her and she simply let them happen, as though she had trained to be hopeless, now there is a feeling that she is in control of her own destiny, even though the destiny in question is pretty appalling.

So we climb up Smallpox Hill. I knew it would be Smallpox because this is her favourite place. What she doesn't know is that it's also my favourite place. From the top you can see everything, I sometimes think: everything at least that has any bearing on my world. It is the summit, the centre of my landscape, so that it can be seen from anywhere that I go. From it you can see the limits of my life. It's not so small when you look. If there was such a thing as our own local heaven, it would be on top of Smallpox, except there's no God up here and no gates either unless you count the five bar one that Maria has just jumped over.

The path up is steep and we both struggle in the heat. From the top, the fields up the Herdsley valley and down to Wormbrdge fit together like tessera. Because of the heat it's almost as though everything bar the summit is under water: a light, insubstantial water, just like it used to be millions of years ago before the floods went away.

We sit down exhausted at the top. There is an

avenue of trees that no one is sure who planted and pits in the ground where houses once stood, lived in by the smallpox victims as they slowly died. On the map, there is no official footpath up here. It is meant to be out of bounds except that it isn't. It seems an odd way to have dealt with disease. Send them up to some godforsaken place and pretend they don't exist. Although the world has moved on, in fact smallpox has been officially eradicated, there are still the ill that are hidden away, addicts and alcoholics and people miserable and down trodden, where pustules have become scars of self harm.

I lie back and look at the few clouds moving through the trees above. Then I ask Maria what she wanted to tell me. We sit in the summer grass. She waits a moment before she says anything. I always thought this was the drugs, but I know now that this is the real Maria. She waits before she speaks.

"They want me to apply for life insurance."

I'm expecting more but nothing comes.

"But…but, you'll never get life insurance Maria, I told you that before." I laugh awkwardly.

"Yeah, but they don't know that." She continues without laughing at all. "They want it sorted within three weeks." Then she looks at me straight and very close, so I can see the tiny pores of her skin.

"They're going to kill me, Dr Bradbury, I know they are."

I have dreaded this moment for some time because, although I'm involved in all this, it's not till now that I need to take centre stage. I know they're going to kill Maria too and I know that I will not be able to stand by while they do it.

Even at the height of the day, looking out to the west there is still orange in the sky, as though the pigment is waiting patiently for the end of the day.

"Why you Maria? Why are you on the list? Have you been on a trip to Mexico as well?"

She is sullen and, frankly, I don't blame her. I can have this off hand mood that spurts out all sorts of empty meaningless rhetoric. I feel like I want to start again. How many times do I feel like, if life was a play, I'd keep rewriting what I say and do, because it so often comes out wrong.

"Why you Maria?"

"I dunno," she says and looks where I'm looking, west out over Lower Wormbridge to the Severn, and the Welsh hills and even, if the earth didn't curve so irritatingly, out to the Atlantic to America to Mexico, the Pacific.

Maria looks back at me.

"I suppose I just know too much."

"About what?" I say. I know that to get anywhere here, I need to keep her talking.

"About them, about The Brothers."

I stop and look at her. I've been picking up lots of things about The Brothers. I've caught snatches, but quite quickly snatches are becoming not enough. I need to know more, and at the same time I don't really want to know. I am undergoing the same process that leads me to hide my eyes in a horror film, but not actually leave the room.

"Look Maria, I don't know how you expect me to help against murderers. I'm just a doctor. I'm not

## Smallpox Hill

Jack Bauer; I'm no hero. What did you think I could do?"

She stays silent and looks at me, long, like, just by the looking I might understand what it is I can do. That silence lends my impotence a pathetic shade, like blame, like I am somehow letting her down.

"Do you really think that they intend to kill you?" I say at last.

"Yep." She is never one to waste words, or looks for that matter.

"Why you, all of a sudden?" I say

"I just know too much, that's all."

"Yes but too much about what?"

"Everything."

Two sea gulls, blown inshore by an odd wind, wheel and squawk in the valley between Queens Long Down and us; so white amongst the bleached fields.

"What is everything?" I ask.

"The Brothers; everything."

I stay silent because most people at this point would explain themselves a little more clearly. She stays silent too and we again look out to the view.

"Maria, you need to tell me all about this. If I'm to help out I need to know."

She stays silent again.

I tell her about the phone call last evening, almost verbatim because it has been replayed in my head all night.

"You need to tell me about The Brothers." I say finally.

"Yeah, I suppose you need to know, now that

they've burnt down your house."

"It wasn't my house. It was my girlfriend's or actually my ex-girlfriend's."

I feel like I'm giving too much information here, so I just nod to finish off.

"The Brothers is a stupid name because it's just one man now. The rest are dead." She doesn't look pleased but she doesn't look that sad either.

"Who are The Brothers then?" I get a bit closer to her now. She is anxious and chews something invisible, or moves her lips over her teeth. Then she starts talking again, like she's half way through a conversation.

"Oh, The Brothers, they're Christians, rich Christians. At the beginning there were five of them. Lay preachers you know, like, trying to convert, evangelical. They used to be into saving souls, big time: drug addicts, prostitutes, any fucker would do, as long as they needed saving." She checks to see if the swear words are allowed. She speaks carelessly.

"Saving souls," she goes on, "that and making money on the stock market, spreading the faith."

"And now they want to murder you? I just don't get it"

She nods, slightly impatiently it feels.

"So, hang on, first off they are Christians, right? But then they get into a bit of extortion, is it, or murder, or both. So how can they go from Christians to murder. That's not in the Bible."

Maria looks down at her hands and then up to above the skyline and then sighs. She doesn't look at me but carries on talking. The sun is hot on us in the grass so that a baked smell of vegetation, delicious and full and exotic fills the air.

"So, to start there are five of them and they decide that, as good Christians, they need to help the less well off in society, help them to live a good Christian life. So they round up all the losers, all the addicts, junkies, alcoholics, child prostitutes, paedophiles, everyone that is bad in life as they see it, and they help them, they give them money which they have earned on the stock market, Norman was some sort of broker, and they help these people. They may genuinely have been good to start with, but most of the people they try and save just take stuff until The Brothers stopped giving and then those people fucked off elsewhere. They weren't into the Lord, those junkies. Not ever. They were like all junkies just trying to grab what they could. The Lord had never done much for them. It felt like the feeling was mutual"

I just nod and don't say anything

She nods too, and then she goes on, "So these Brothers are rich, and soon they start diversifying. That's what they call it. When the junkies stop behaving like they wanted them to behave, they get angry. Looking back, I'm not sure they were ever that into God. That was just a cover for some weird ideas about the losers in society. The way the Brothers saw it, they were better off dead, if they weren't going to get converted. Because no one much cared for the addicts, no one misses them when they're dead. So then they start bringing back people from abroad, poor people. They get these weird tastes for things, for people and sex, I don't know…"

She only just finishes her sentence, it stutters to a halt like an old tube train.

"What, like prostitutes?" I say.

"Yeah, but they're young see. They're babies, they don't know. The Brothers show them the Lord and what they have to do for His respect."

"What, from Mexico?"

"Yeah, mostly Indian kids. Later on anyway. Chiapas, where the families are poor."

The wind gets up briefly, as though it's listening and suddenly remembers it needs to breath.

"Except it didn't start with foreign kids. It started with me. The stepfather and fucking Clive and that man sitting in hospital, Norman, while all the time mum just sits in the next room sipping white wine."

There is a long and difficult silence, mostly because I have no idea what to say next.

"And they want to kill you because you know? You know what they're like, is that it?"

"Yeah. Partly"

"And Paul told you some of this?"

"Nah, I've known this shit for years. I would have warned him but he was already involved when I met him."

"So," I'm trying to piece this together as I go, "So, you've known for ages. Have they just found out that you know?"

"No, I think they just felt for me or something. It was with Paul, I suppose, what happened with Paul and me knowing full well what happened and then you sticking your great fucking foot in it with the pathologist and the insurance company. So Norman starts acting all strange. Everyone is scared, everyone. You start asking difficult questions. He's got this operation, he's scared. He changes so quickly. Like the way he went weird with the Christian business. He can be like an animal, one that seems well enough behaved and then goes berserk."

She stops talking and looks vaguely out again at the sky and Wales. A hot wind comes up from below us.

"So he is The Brothers?"

"Yeah. He killed the rest of them, one by one, or he just paid Clive to do it. Hence the big fuck off car."

"So, the prick that rang, last night, the ex-friend of your ex-stepfather, he isn't a Brother?"

"God no! That's Clive. He's just a prick."

"And your ex-stepfather?"

She nods, "He was the first Brother to go. He pissed off Norman big time by mixing it up with boys and a bit of stealing. I can't remember much except when he realised what was happening, his shit scared face as he left the house early. He never came back, thank fucking Christ."

I think for a while. The wind raises the tree leaves as though the whole of nature is painted on a sheet that is being raised by invisible arms.

"What I don't get is why you're still alive, now, and why they've decided after all this time, that they want you gone."

"Suppose they felt I'd suffered enough."

She looks down at her arms and I look down. Something is shifting within me. Some realisation.

"So why now?"

"Maybe it's the money, from Paul, that should have been his; maybe it's just him, maybe it's just him feeling vulnerable. Maybe it's being ill that's making him feel vulnerable. I don't know, maybe he wants to go to heaven. Mostly though, it's you. Your sniffling around has spooked him. Soon as you start acting suspicious, then the insurance company begin asking questions, and he hates that, he really hates that. And then he sort of wants to be good as well, I think, in some warped way. He wants to clear away everyone who knows he is an evil man, so that he can go to heaven"

"What, by killing more people?"

"Look I don't know why he's acting out like this. I just know he is. It's not what I would call Christian, but then that's never stopped anyone in the past has it. Anyway, how do I know why anyone does anything? How do I know why people do what they do? Everything is confusing."

I nod because it's not my idea of ensuring a welcome up in heaven, either. I'm trying desperately to think where all this stuff leaves us, Maria and me, and to be honest, it sounds like we're fucked, as Maria would put it

"So," I say slowly again, " He is the Brothers and has become ill and needs an operation, while Clive cleans up everything, including you."

She stops me with her hand and makes to say something and then doesn't, and then she continues, as though she is speaking her thoughts to herself. "Everyone's been saying that over time he's just got more and more paranoid. First of all he killed off the brothers, one by one, because he wanted all the money to himself. He thought they were plotting against him, and I don't know maybe they were. But I'm not sad about that, they deserved all they got. That was when he hit on the life insurance idea and making himself the next of kin. They were brothers after all." She laughs in a hollow way that isn't funny.

"He's in total control now. He don't let anything slip. He's careful with detail. I think that's why he is so angry with me. He feels like it's his money. He came up with this brainwave idea of insuring junkies, when they had ceased being useful to him, and then having them killed. Not only does it rid him of all that scum in society, he even makes money. But I stole one on him, without him knowing. As though he doesn't owe me anything for fucking up my whole life…" Then, silently she starts crying again. I put my arm around her. I say something stupid like, "It'll be ok."

She stops crying and pulls away from me. "No, it fucking won't!"

I look down and try slowly to lure her back. There is a stony silence again between us.

"Look Maria, I think we have to go to the police. They can't ignore all this, all this stuff you've said about."

"Don't you understand. You've seen what the Police are like. They know where their bread is buttered. And as for me. Me! My evidence! They'll just laugh at me, even if they weren't bent. I'm mad after all. I've been in that psychiatric ward thirty times at least, the only place where they have guards called nurses, guards to stop me getting out and others getting in. But you? Who knows, they might listen. You can try if you want." She looks up and to the right, effortlessly and then she starts chewing something and moving her lips over her teeth again.

She stays silent. Silence is Maria's weapon, that and Stanley knives and threats of suicide. That's about all she's got and I'm thinking that all things considered, she's used them pretty well so far.

It's slow, but I'm beginning to see what we are up against here.

"So, that explains Dr Cape."

"Yes and that Policeman who you hate and the junky upstairs. Norman hates being weak. So it will be me, definitely, and most likely you as well, now you've stuck your stupid nose into all this. I warned you at the start, you could have avoided this. Unfortunately I was born into it, it's my birthright to be abused."

"So," I ask, "was Paul an addict?"

"No, never. He might have done a bit of stealing, once or twice, but Paul was a good man. "

"How come he got mixed up with the Brothers, then?"

"He needed some money, quickly. And he hadn't met me by then. So I couldn't warn him. He had done one run for them. But then he realised what was up and refused to do any more. And Norman got really angry. He called it a betrayal. The main problem was that now Paul knew all about his horrible business interests so Paul had to go. I feel like I should have stopped it somehow. But I couldn't. I couldn't stop it even though I knew it was coming….Its been a long struggle just protecting myself for Gods sake….." She starts crying again and this time its copious and loud and I feel all the suffering in her coming out in great streams.

At this point she suddenly screams at the top her voice "Fucking Norman Waye, I hate you." And then she goes back to crying, but its steadier by now.

She tails off and the silence returns, apart from an occasional sob that escapes. We stand up and lean against a tree. I hug her because, I don't know, it just seems the right thing to do. The insects are making inroads and trace out their paths through the air.

I am trying desperately to think of a way out of this: a way to save Maria from her fate and change everything so I can start living my life again. Herdsley Peak, the volcano I imagine it to be, seems alive in the haze. The River Severn shows like a ribbon of silver drawn from an artists' irregular pen. I'm thinking about killdeer and locked psychiatric wards and that maybe in the past this would be about when Maria went off on one of her cutting frenzies: cutting and cutting until I have to section her.

Then the idea comes to me. It would be simple to get Maria holed up in the psychiatric hospital with its guards, or nurses, and the great blanket that is the NHS to wrap around her. I tell her about it, I say lets just admit you to Fairmead, but she starts laughing again, and this time it's at me, like she finds me funny and faintly stupid.

"First thing is," she says, "what about you? Second thing is, the consultant said he would never section me again, I wasn't worth it or something, and so it wouldn't be on a restricted ward. I'd have no protection at all." She makes this sneering expression like this is a playground and she is a sort of bully. Then she says something like, hang on, and begins thinking about something else.

It's uncomfortable and the wind from the Bristol Channel decides it's time that it arrived and lifts the branches right up like they are waving. There are pits in the ground, just past the trees that were once huddled in by smallpox victims waiting to die but are now grassed over so that they just look weird and faintly archaeological, a reminder from something in the past. Down at the end of this valley, next to the Severn, another family doctor famously injected a boy and then exposed him to smallpox. Now every one remembers that name Jenner. What will they be remembering me for? The doctor who fucked up and let his patients die, who got too involved, who hasn't really done anything that's worth remembering? Dr Bradbury: what will they say about him?

Maria is still looking at her feet and I'm sort of getting self-obsessed and maudlin and I feel increasingly confused.

So we have come to this.

We run down the hill in the end. The sun is still piercing like small bright white knives. The running helps me and I can hear Maria wheezing slightly but just behind. She comes up level and then, unexpectedly she grabs my hand and we run down like that. I hold on tight to her like we are children. There is that feeling of careening down a hill a little out of control that I love. I keep thinking of the sort of childhood Maria had and I'm really not sure if she's ever run down a hill, holding someone's hand like this.

# CHAPTER TWELVE

By the time I get back to the surgery, they've already killed Julian.

Just while I was sitting up on Smallpox - looking out over the very house on Queens Hill, nestled beneath Limcombe, the last headland of the Cotswolds - there was Julian getting killed. If my eyesight was good enough I could have even seen the killing taking place, through the bedroom window.

Like some dream, I seem to have developed an inability to move or do anything useful or have any idea of time, or perhaps timing. I'm getting everything wrong and now someone else has died.

I get back to the surgery and I try and phone Rosie at her Mum's house, but instead I get her mum, who isn't helpful. She treats me like a criminal, someone whose daughter needs protection from.

## Smallpox Hill

Julian is up in his room, out on the bed, when I arrive. It's the same bed that the forgotten junkie and Paul have died in. The room has become a sort of killing room that, in addition, is getting nastily familiar to me. Maybe it's just the paintwork that kills them: the orange is particularly horrible and it's raised and textured by some glyptic paper that's meant to be, I think, urns with flowers stuffed in the top.

Maria is with Bernard, downstairs, standing on the front lawn next to the old pushchair, which some well-meaning police officer has righted. It's like a little reception committee, as though I'm about to open a new classroom or launch a ship. The Police are there, the little twat in his slightly tight trousers and an older man who I haven't seen before.

Work is stacking up back at the surgery; I'm losing grip, ever so slowly, on all of it, so I decide that this will have to be quick: confirm death, ring coroner get back as soon as possible.

Then the young officer says, "Isn't it a bit suspicious, all your young patients dying like this?"

I'm nearly floored because, I'm pretty sure that if anyone's a paid up member of the Brothers, it will be Mr Macho here.

I agree with him that I find it very suspicious. Then this slow truculent grin starts to spread on his face, slick like and burlesque.

"Yeah, you should take more care of them, don't you think Kev?"

The older one barely even acknowledges this

question. The young one laughs at what he's said.

I take a look at Julian. He's only wearing underpants and somehow his expression, even when dead, still has that slacker's appeal, that down sizing, uncaring sneer.

A laptop lies open next to his bed. He still has the remnants of his Mexican holiday tan: he is a sort of Cancun orange, but maybe that's the wallpaper. He has a white mark where his watch was and also marks where his flip-flop straps crossed his feet. I inadvertently think of Louise and the thin straps of her flip-flops. I hate the way my brain works sometimes.

The younger officer stands in one corner, like a security man, which in a jacked up sense, he is. I go through the motions: check pulse, heart, and eyes. He hasn't been dead that long: his skin still has a mild tension, before it goes solid. I manage to include the feet in my general examination, something that I've never done before, because, quite honestly, there's not usually much point looking at a dead man's feet.

It's tiny but it is there: a small injection mark, just above the big toe.

I start talking to the younger cop again. It becomes clear that there is not an ounce of compassion or sadness for him about death. It's as though he's at a minor car accident. The issues are the same, the need to complete the paperwork, make sure it's done to the book.

Then he says, "There's rumours flying around about you Doc: matches and petrol, does that mean anything, punching a poor old man in the face, any bells doctor?"

I'm on my guard big time here. I need some mighty fine acting to get myself out of this one. "Oh God," I say, "Is that what's being said about me?"

I must keep asking questions.

"Yep," he replies, "except left to me, I would get you to change your name. Dr Shipman might be better."

I look at him cold and about as nasty as I can manage. "What are you saying?"

I should have practised in front of the mirror or something because it doesn't have the desired effect.

"I'm just saying that I wonder if you should change your name by deed poll to Dr Shipman."

"Why?" I say, "Why would you call me that? I'm quite fond of Dr Bradbury, actually."

"It's just the rate at which your patients die, particularly the poorer ones and the drug addicts."

I look at him incredulous. I know where he is trying to lead this and I need to act surprised.

Then, by chance, a message comes through on his radio and he turns to the window to talk. I take out my mobile, move as close as I can to Julian, and take a couple of pictures of his foot.

He finishes talking and turns slowly around so that he can mock me some more. However, I decide that mockery is not why I'm doing this particular job and put my things back in my bag. I hide behind my profession sometimes. It can be one of my most useful moves.

As I'm leaving though, he calls after me. "We're expecting you down the station, this afternoon. You've got some explaining to do."

I stop for a moment and he stops.

"In fact, I'm not sure you're even fit to practice as a doctor."

I smile at him. I can smile at anyone.

The surgery is quiet enough. I phone the coroner from there. I realise it's useless, but I tell him all my suspicions, even about Dr Cape, and also the injection mark in the foot and how I'm sure this man has been murdered. He asks me whether I discussed this with the police. I tell him no, and he suggests this might be an idea.

I want to shout that I can't go to the police, but he really would think me mad and not fit to practice if I told him that.

I'm determined that somehow, if the authorities see what is happening, then in the end, this will all turn out fine and I'll be safe, and I'll be back with Rosie, and Maria will be back to normal: stealing pills from under the push chair and getting doped.

But I'm losing will. This is what happens when the mighty fall. I'm losing confidence and will. The coroner is sounding doubtful. Doctors playing detective must have rich fantasy lives. All the so-called evidence is so thin that I sometimes feel that perhaps I am making all of this up.

I try Rosie and get her mother again. This woman is hard and controlling and I can tell she will never let me speak to Rosie, not under any circumstances. I want to say that it wasn't me; you must believe me. Then I realise that I will have to say that I was shagging Louise all night; I didn't have the time.

Next I phone Louise, but instead I also get her mother. What is it about me? Mother says that Louise has gone away for a few days, but she should ring tonight and she can give a message to phone me at home, I give my name and telephone number.

I'm getting this pressing, hollowed-out headache. It's because I didn't sleep last night, I know. I can barely concentrate but I cruise through afternoon surgery. I keep thinking about how I am just trying to prevent dying, nothing more. It's all quite simple. Except that it becomes increasingly unsimple. And it's not to prevent, after all, but only the delay in dying I can hope for.

It must be my lack of sleep. I am ruminating about the meaning of things, the differences between right and wrong, reality and fiction, love and hatred. Are there absolute rights or is everything shaded in some sort of difficult ethic?

A man my age comes in with a bad back. There are all sorts of patients who come and unload their differing problems on me. The funny thing today is that I envy them, everyone one of them. I'd love to just have a bad back.

---

At the police station Kev, the older officer, is on duty. He reads up some notes from the day before.

"So," he says, "the jilted lover story was it?"

"No" I say.

"So why did you do it?" He is nearly as bad as the young cocky one, is Kevin, but also slightly less intelligent.

"I didn't do it. Why do you think I did it?"

"Your footprints everywhere, a good motive, even some finger prints."

"She was my girlfriend, I practically lived with her, no wonder there are some prints around there."

"Yeah, but she decided that she didn't like you. What happened?" he starts reading the incident report card. "So, as far as I can see, Doctor, you caught her kissing another man in a car."

I just nod although inside is a hot liquid of anger. Is it my imagination or are the Police trying to wind me up here? Yes, and sort of enjoying the detail perhaps a little too much.

"I'm glad you've got it so well documented, I've got it documented as well." I bang on my chest, indicating my heart in a rather tacky movement that I immediately regret.

"Look," Kevin goes on, "you're in trouble here because you're the only person that the owner of the cottage has any sort of dispute with."

"Yes, I know, I know," I answer. "It's just that I was with another woman that night and I really don't want Rosie to get to know about it."

"Will she corroborate your story?"

"Yes, of course she will," I say.

Kevin looks down at the notes in front of him. "Well, that might change things a little."

"I bloody hope so, because I didn't burn the house down, in fact I've never done anything violent or destructive like this in my whole life."

"That's odd," Kevin says. "I've got another report of you physically abusing an old man outside your surgery yesterday. Luckily for you, he didn't press charges or try and report you; this is eyewitness evidence only. Otherwise, with all the witnesses, you would have been up for GBH."

Kevin is in his forties with battleship grey, uniform grey hair and a hard face and a very, very slender trace of a northern accent, the sort of trace that gets stronger when people are drinking. He is dour, and I am waiting on his judgement, it feels like. You know you have lost control of your life when you are waiting, or your fate is waiting, on a man like this.

"That man's been watching me for about a month. My patients are getting murdered and I'm beginning to work out what is going on. This man follows me and reports back to…to…." Oh God, I've said too much. "That's why I punched him. They were trying to burn down my house. They thought I was living with Rosie, because I spend a lot of time up there, and they got confused and decided it was my house."

Kevin holds his hand up.

I've been through enough, and I'm finally cracking. I've got to tell someone; it's just that I wish I hadn't blabbed to Kevin.

"Shall we start from the beginning and this time, much more slowly."

"Look," I say, desperate now to find a way out: I'm too tired for all this and my headache is thudding like a nodding donkey in the desert. "Look, I've been working really hard and I think I'm cracking up a little. Just forget what I've said."

"You seem upset," Kevin says, "do you want to make a statement?"

"Yes, can I make a statement about spending the night with Louise?"

"Well, its up to you."

Kevin is playing another lethal game. He is somehow allowing me to spool out enough rope so that I can simply hang myself, all the time pretending that he is trying to stop it happening. A smiling death, an entrapment that is elegant and leaves him intact and in the right. The games people, or at least policeman play. I could write a whole book about it.

But he also might be a good cop: my salvation, my last hope, the man who somehow stops me from descending into a type of hell. It's just that I've no way of knowing. The trouble is, if I get it wrong, then The Brothers will know everything that I know. They talk about knowledge as a weapon. It will turn into a loaded gun, or more accurately a loaded syringe, with Maria and me at the end of its two barrels, or needles or whatever.

So I duck out. If he is the bad cop, I haven't burnt my boats completely.

I make a statement and give Louise's full name and our activities on the night in question.

It's easy when it's done.

He looks at me a little strange, when I leave. I don't really blame him.

I go home and try and phone Rosie again. Her mother answers and asks whether I'm going to harass her daughter for the rest of her life. She is the complete matriarch: magnificent and fearsome and protective to the point of being stultifying. What does Rosie want, that's what I want to ask her? I tell her that the police are aware that I have an alibi and anyway it's not something I'd do, this arson business. She cuts me short and puts the phone down.

I speak to Claude for a few minutes. He is busy, going to some band but I need to talk. He says that my life is rich, which I find strange. Why does he suddenly think that my life is rich? Perhaps it's a language thing.

He contends that the true essence of life - the business end, the crux - is that we are alive and then that we die, and that, in itself, gives all human life its tension. I agree with him but I also think, so what? He says, so, you're living properly, to which I tell him, I would prefer to live superficially, perhaps down in Bradley Stoke (that Claude jokes is named after me), in a modern super-fitted 70's double garaged three bedroom just detached special.

That's what it is: I want to be detached, that's what I've lost, I've become too involved in life.

Claude tells me I need a break. I agree with him. He tells me he is picking me up and we are heading for West Wales. I protest that I've got surgeries and I'll let people down.

Claude is wise, he is the professor after all - as well as the confessor - and I know he's right.

So I ring Sue and tell her that I'm losing the plot and I need a few days off and could she find a locum for the morning. She says something snide like it won't make much difference if I'm there or not, by implication suggesting that I'm a lazy shit who doesn't pull his weight. Yet she would never actually say as much. It as though she is playing a sort of fill-in-the-missing-words game.

Claude is right: it's just what I need. The heat is continuing and the sun beats down all day, like fingers drumming on my skin. We take books and wine and sun cream and tents and that's about it. Marloes beach at low tide is like an aquarium. The rocks are made from madder root and the sea is like emeralds from close-up and sapphire from further away.

We body surf and talk and read and drink. Sometimes I think these are all the things I need to survive. Perhaps a bit of food as well.

Coming home, I'm nervous. Nervous that some calamity, some vestiges of my increasing number of problems will be waiting for me.

But there's nothing, just a pile of unsolicited mail.

It's only the next morning when I get into work that it finally hits. There is a letter in my box; it says my contract has been rejected: I have no job.

They've already changed the passwords on the computer to deny me access.

# CHAPTER THIRTEEN

I've thought of a few scenarios that might just happen to me, culminating in me getting killed in an unpleasant way, or raped by some horrible slimy balding men, but for some reason I've never imagined being sacked, losing my job.

These new contracts, they are usually issued without thinking in a routine manner, the only barrier is the paperwork (unless you've been absolutely awful or had sex with one of your patients or have become a junky), otherwise it should be plain and simple.

It isn't plain and simple now. It's got hugely more complicated. The receptionists can't believe it either. There is a nice little moment of pandemonium when everyone is talking at once and the queue of patients stretches out of the door like a toy snake painted in many different colours.

I just can't get my head around this. The

manager calls the health department because, although I've been losing it these last few days, there's never been a problem before. It takes about an hour to get through to anyone who might know something. I notice, in the waiting room, that the man who I hit a few days before is loitering. I take a close look at him. Having been convinced that he was a spy for the Brothers, I now wonder about him. His face looks gentle although there is some asymmetry to it, some irregularity. It's just like these bastards not to press charges. It sort of doesn't give me a chance, but in addition there's something not quite right with him. He is dressed so bizarrely for a start, and always he appears in the same clothes. I'm sure he must live out of a tent up Breakfast Hill, behind the town, where the travellers hang out until some stroppy resident complains and they are cleared out. I regret what I did to him. I feel like I regret plenty but sitting back waiting for the director of personnel to finish his meeting so he can tell me why I'm sacked, I realise that hitting him is the only thing I regret, the only thing I would change, given the chance to do all this again.

Finally, I am put through to the director. He is so terribly charming: what an awful shock etc etc, but I remember throughout that it is him who has made this final decision. There are specialists at these games, sharing your shock and outrage and a dreadful decision that they have a hand in making. I'm feeling as though most people are out to get me, so it's not really paranoia because it's true. There's Rosie's Mum and Rosie, the young prick of a policemen, there's the Brothers and his henchman, there's Sue at the practice and finally there's this director who is very sorry and how awful.

Perhaps I've done something fatal here a few weeks ago: angered some super powerful God, walked under some especially dangerous ladder crossed my legs at the wrong time. Because, everywhere I turn, they are against me. I suppose that I'm rather making a drama out of this. There's still Claude and my Mum who don't seem to be out to get me, them and maybe Louise, although now she's got to admit to the world that she spent a night with me, it might turn out nasty as well.

The director says that it will be necessary to reapply and attend a hearing and the earliest I can work is 3 months time. It's just the process you see, awfully longwinded.

I ask him whether I might be able to know why this wasn't passed, why I'm not getting a new contract.

He audibly shuffles and clears his throat. He begins by telling me that other doctors have been worried about my mental state. So that'll be Sue. There was an assault outside the surgery, apparently, but the main problems centre around the Police and some other interested parties who feel performance is significantly impaired. There was an episode a few days go when I apparently was seen becoming indecently involved with a patient, on top of a hill, a local beauty spot. I ask about interested parties but he is terribly sorry, for legal reasons this is all he is allowed to say. He feels sure -

he has a horrible ingratiating way of saying sure, like shourer - he feels sure that it is all a misunderstanding and that it will only take a few weeks really to straighten everything out.

I feel him trying to wind up this conversation, but with that consummate skill of the master manager: so smooth and seamless you barely notice that he is trying to wriggle out of his responsibilities.

In reality, I know there's nothing I can say. If I rant and start shouting this will only reinforce his argument. If I say nothing then nothing will happen. So I say nothing because, there's nothing to say. I could say that I'm competent and that I'm very popular with patients. But patients don't know anything.

After he's put the phone down, ever so gently, I am overwhelmed by a feeling that I'm not right, I'm not fit enough to do this job. The way I've been behaving is not appropriate for this profession. How could I become so involved? How could I care so much? It seems strange to me that, having been so cold, so efficient, so capable of allowing the pressures of this job to pass by me, it's at the moment when I stick my neck out and try and do something good, worthwhile, try and properly influence events rather than just record them and listen attentively, this is what has done for me.

A year ago I wouldn't allow this to have gone on and I certainly wouldn't have run down the field holding hands with Maria.

I feel my face and rub my hair that still contains sand from the Atlantic breakers in fine tiny chards.

My mind is blank. I really truly do not know what to do.

A receptionist brings me coffee. I hear from the front desk the patients being told that I no longer work but they have a new doctor, Dr Craig, who is very nice. It's surprising how quickly you can be forgotten. I walk over to my box, to have a final clear out.

On the top virtually is the form from the Insurance Company about Maria. There's also a note written by one of the receptionists asking me to phone Maria, quite urgent it says, whatever that means. I calculate that I have about a week before the company informs the Brothers that no life insurance is possible, and then, that will be the end of Maria. I think of what she's said, of the Brother sitting in The Royal hospital awaiting his operation, of the time ticking and then of me. I know too much, I am too involved.

This thought, although not new, dawns on me like I have just come across it. It floods over me, like it is liquid that is being poured liberally.

I'm really not thinking straight. Maybe it's time to disappear completely; I can take Maria with me, we can wait. The man might die during the operation. Then the problems will be over.

I finish my box, walk upstairs to the room where we have our coffee and meetings but which is now empty since I'm meant to be downstairs seeing patients. On the computer in that room I do a search for Norman Waye. Plenty comes up, a couple of newspaper articles about him being cleared of murder, one article about making money from stock, helping drug addicts, and then it all strangely goes quiet about 10 yrs ago, there is nothing new about him at all. There is a picture of him, on images, and he is standing with Clive, the great fat faced self satisfied lump. Norman himself is much more handsome, with grey hair that's very full, not receding at all, and smooth, refined.

I phone Maria. She sounds like she's in bed. It's only a short phone call: I don't trust phones and clearly she doesn't either. We arrange to meet and then I give her my home number. I'm not really sure why.

When I go downstairs my box, that I've just emptied, has, for some reason, got an apple in it. I ask the receptionists and they haven't put it there. I ask them if anyone has been in and they say no, but to be honest, they are not really listening.

I look at the apple. It is red as a cricket ball on one side and green on the other. I put it in my pocket. My imagination is really not healthy.

I keep thinking of Rosie. I long for Rosie, a long visceral longing, as though I hadn't realised how much I loved her until now. I remember tucking her into the freshly made bed at my house. That was the last I saw of her. I think her Mother, who has always disliked me, has decided this is a watershed and that she will make sure that the nasty pill pusher is not allowed anymore to sully the company of her especial daughter. In fact the watershed occurred when her daughter started snogging the local undertaker in a pub car park, but she almost certainly doesn't know that particular watershed.

You see how my mind is. It's intent on torturing itself.

I need to go home.

The trouble is, I'm beginning to doubt myself. It's as though I'm slipping deeper into some dirty Amsterdam canal, spiralling down. It's the final straw, not in itself that damning, just a sensation of ripping and I feel all clichéd up, like I'm a camel and have a back for loading. I feel unexpectedly dazed.

I wonder to myself if it's just that I'm ill, ill like everyone else who comes to see me. Except it doesn't feel like anything a doctor could do much about. Unless they could transport me out of here. Get my job back. And Rosie, then sort out these Brothers and somehow cancel out how I've behaved. Now that would be something. That's a doctor I'd like to meet.

I think I just want to disappear completely. The way I see it, though, reality precludes this, and anyway, it's never been worth burying your head, especially if you're a camel. Even I can see that, and it feels comforting that I still have a modicum of sense left.

Even so, I make a few phone calls, grab my stuff from underneath Dr Craig's feet and just get out. The receptionist says goodbye but there is something different about how they talk to me. That's the trouble, when doubt enters it is contagious, even if unfounded, and spreads and becomes somehow a fact, a reality in itself.

I can see that they don't absolutely disbelieve that I am in serious trouble.

And they're right.

When I get home the phone is ringing; it's Maria. I must unplug the phone I realise even though I've given her my number. Maria is short as usual. He is having his operation tomorrow. Then she waits. I can hear her voice cracking to reveal impatience and a vicious temper. She manages to keep this under control. I tell her I will ring her tomorrow afternoon. Maria has a new side that I haven't seen before: she is petulant and wilful. She is scared and her way out of fear is aggression.

I phone Mum. She speaks to me slowly and carefully like she always does. I have to tell her everything. I am her only child and she covets me almost to the point of incarceration. I was actually her fifth pregnancy, but the previous four ended far too early, miscarried. Consequently, not only am I especial to her, I feel as though I need to live the lives of the other four siblings who didn't make it out; live it for them.

Dad died two years ago. He was tense, Dad was. They always blamed it on the war, all those dead bodies seen at such an early age, all that intimations of mortality. He couldn't actually leave his house for the last three months. He was too terrified. I've only ever spoken to Mum about this but I see him, sitting in his chair, smoking and smoking, his muscles hard with tension.

After he died, Mum met another man. He was

## Smallpox Hill

good for her; he had lots of little hobbies: he liked to write dialogue and would send in script after script to the BBC, although he never got much response. He loved kites and old houses and gardens and did odd things like collected miniature butterflies. She was happy with him. The only problem was she had stupidly seen a clairvoyant after Dad's death who told her she would fall in love with another man but she mustn't go with him, there was disaster at the end.

So, she turned down his repeated requests for marriage and a shared life, and in the end he went off with someone else.

So here she is and I tell her they've cancelled my contract and I'm out of work and a bit stressed and a bit about Rosie's house burning down and the police and how Rosie and I have split.

She never liked Rosie and she sounds pleased. In fact she's never liked any of my girlfriends. It's as though it's some personal affront.

As I talk to her on the phone, the man who I punched walks past, well sort of shuffles past. He looks in at me. I tell mum to hang on and rush out into the lane but by the time I get there, he's gone. I run down to the bottom, where the streams floods in the winter but there is no trace of him. So I run back up and continue the conversation with Mum.

I really do want to talk to this man. He is clearly watching me. He obviously watched me up to Rosie's house, and then either he or one of his mates burnt it down. He was the one who reported me to the powers that be for running downhill holding Maria's hand. How I regret that particularly. It's almost as though I'm trying to set myself up, like I don't need any help from anyone to cock up everything.

I just wish I hadn't hit him, that's all. Through all of life there has to be some unbreakable moral laws. Otherwise I will end up indistinguishable from the Brothers themselves. One of those laws is that you shouldn't punch anyone in the face. I think of that regret as I make coffee and lie out in the hot unending lidless sun. Inside me there is a horrible game going on that I would dearly like to stop. How can I escape this one? How can I survive and go back to before? The more I think about it the less sure I am. Then I think of Paul and Julian and that sad drug addict that have all shared - serially shared - that sad bedroom.

My natural instinct is to run. That's what viscerally I want to do. I want to run away with Maria, to another country, where the Brothers don't have henchmen. I settle on this for a few hours and look through an old Explore magazine, gazing down at pictures of South India and Morocco. Then I drink a whole bottle of wine; smoke about a packet of cigarettes.

I cook a half-hearted meal, watch TV, and listen to music. Still this hunted feeling will not leave. I dip into the second bottle of wine, get about half way down and then finally manage to pass out.

I wake up early. I feel dreadful both mentally and physically. The colour for this one, this Marcus

## Smallpox Hill

canvas is definitely green, green and a harrowing purple circle.

I am intent on escape. I am going to phone Maria and tell her that's it's time to run.

Two things change my mind. To escape, it's generally recognised that you need a means of escaping. I was planning on my car. My lovely Skoda. It's just that there's a problem with my Skoda, a problem that wasn't there yesterday. Someone has decided to redecorate the bodywork using a rather blunt instrument. All four doors are caved in. It's sort of amateur and not very well done. It is surprising that they don't just grab me and inject me, like they did Paul and Julian. I think for a moment that perhaps they don't really want to kill me.

I am thinking at about 100mph, although what that means I'm not sure. I think more accurately I have about a hundred ideas all entering my brain at once. They are trying to freak me, spook me, so that I run off. They are trying deliberately to scare me away, otherwise they would just kill me. So why do something like this? It's naff and sort of old fashioned. It doesn't feel like the work of a supremely powerful organisation. It just doesn't feel how the Brothers normally operate. It's just not slick enough.

Then I think, maybe its something to do with the man I punched - the weird looking one - some sort of personal revenge. It could be one of Rosie's mad family members. As I make this list in my head, I realise how many enemies I seem to have made.

I walk, instead down to the shop to get myself bread and a paper. This is when the second thing happens.

On the billboard of The Citizen - a local paper - in black letters, is news that 'Doctor takes own life.' I am vaguely interested although, with these new contracts I know how they feel.

I buy bread and then I buy The Citizen and sit on the bench outside, facing south, my head in the sun.

Doctors commit suicide all the time, it's a stressful job and they know how to do it properly. None of this thirty paracetamol and have your stomach pumped by some sadistic casualty staff nurse. They go for known remedies. The shock of it is, the doctor in question is Dr Cape.

I read greedily, two or three times. Apparently he was found in his house, where he lived alone, with a syringe in his hand that is believed to have contained insulin although the exact cause of death had not been confirmed. The short biography revealed that he had trained at the same medical school as me, had become a pathologist and now just did police work. He was not married and had no children.

Whether it was the not being married bit, or the medical school bit but I began imaging that it wasn't Dr Cape who had killed himself but me. Except that I know, and although 'know' is a strong word implying absolute truth, I am using it on purpose. I know that Dr Cape didn't kill himself.

His only problem was that he knew too much.

Well he was a rude and insufferable man, as well, there were probably other problems too, but his main problem was that he knew too much of what had gone on. That, as well as the fact that the Brothers were clearly in a panic. The problem is that I know too much as well. And yet somehow I don't know enough either.

At home I do a search for Norman Waye. I feel like I'm looking, slightly desperately, amongst the figments and signs, for something definitive and categorical. Being a doctor is a little like gliding around a darkened room with some prior knowledge of the furniture but not enough to fully navigate your way through. I do find a couple of items, one about a Christian Stockbroker. It feels like this is one big oxymoron. However capitalism isn't immoral, after all, just amoral. There is some old stuff from the press that obviously been planted by some sycophant. Helping the worst off in society. There is no sign of a descent into depravity. What, though, am I expecting; a body count, on line.

There is nothing in all this that contradicts Maria's voicing of events. Only, there is not enough proof, or certainty, that would even flutter a young policeman's eyelashes. So I continue on in doubt, a doubt madam, a man who might never know, fully, about anything. I think for a moment that I have chosen the wrong career. I would like at this moment to be caged by certainty, like an accountant or a mathematician. Numbers have a finite quality.

So there it is, I know too little, and at the same

time too much. Way too much about Norman Waye, I think to myself. I just dearly wish I didn't. I wonder briefly whether it's possible to un-know something and then I feel, there in the sunlight, suddenly very, very scared. There can be no other excuse. Like I said, when an animal is cornered and terrified, it's quite common that aggression is the first emotion, the first instinct. I feel angry like I've never felt before. Something huge and uncontrolled, something that rolls up all the blows that I have been dealt, gathers their energies and spews it all out again like a roar. Anger fills me up and soaks into every corner of myself. Rough unadulterated anger.

And anger is such a blind passion.

## CHAPTER FOURTEEN

I suppose I do feel anger. A great torrent as though it has just been waiting there, waiting for its moment to rush out.

I feel anger on a world level, like I am the United Nations spokesman who sees the poverty and unfairness of the world. Anger by proxy, if you like, and then a real fanatical anger.

Why does it all have to be like this? What fatal step have we taken that so much hate can come out? Where exactly is it coming from? Why do people do inexcusable things for money? There's big pharma and bankers and the Brothers. What really do they think they are trying to do? Why do men want to have sex with children? Why does someone think it's ok to threaten me on the phone and burn down other people's houses?

I'm just trying to be good, and so maybe sometimes I cock up, but I have never picked up a hard thing and damaged anything like someone has done to my car.

I drink a second cup of coffee and take off my shirt. Insects bother me. To be honest everything bothers me.

I smoke two cigarettes in quick succession, and then make two phone calls. The first is to Maria, I tell her about the car. She says she knows. She sounds even more on edge than me. We arrange to meet in ten minutes time.

The second call is to the hospital. I speak to the ward sister, briefly, because she is a type of briefly person, all her words are snipped off at the end, like she is not wanting to waste an ounce of mouth energy.

Only one door of the car opens, and it's one of the back ones, so I have to clamber over the back rests to get to the drivers seat, as though I've broken in. It drives fine, but everyone stops what they're doing and stares as I drive past. It's strange but someone smashing up this car has done nothing to me, because I realise I never really liked it anyway. All the windows are full of the remains of broken glass, but the wind comes in and it's so warm that, balm like, it sooths me and I feel oddly relaxed. It always feels good to be moving, physically moving and anyway, at least now I'm going somewhere even if it's only to Alan's down on the old Bristol Road, after I've met up with Maria

I stop at the foot of Smallpox Hill, by the gate, and wait for the earthy roar of Maria's Mercedes.

When you're waiting, time does all sorts of odd

contortions. It gets all sort of elongated until the person arrives and then that very same bit of time gets squashed together again, concertinaed, so afterwards its seems like nothing. Except before she arrives it feels like a whole lake full of time that I spend.

She gets out and climbs the gate and we are walking up the path surrounded by bracken unfurled in the heat and smelling bracken-ish and slightly like the sea. Old oaks lean sideways and have beefsteak fungus growing from their roots. This time, instead of sitting on the top, she finds a tree stump that someone once has cut into a chair. It has room for both of us but it's high up so that neither of our legs reach the floor and hang beneath us swinging with nerves like we are children. There is the stink of an old kicked over fire from some weeks ago and then the slope takes off alarmingly, like we are on top of a wave that at any time we will slide down.

It's difficult today. It's not so much a stony silence, more the quietness of the hopeless, a silent despair. It's like she is waiting for me to say something and I am doing the same.

Finally I crack. In psychological therapies there is a technique called sweating it out, where you try and stay silent until one of you has to speak. It's meant to be a way of making sure that only the most important stuff comes out, the things that can't be kept inside.

"What are we going to do, Maria?"

There is silence at that moment and there is only

the wind, still from the west and the buzz of the air all about us.

"Let's just hope he dies in the operation. There's always the chance of that."

The silence comes back, and like children sitting obediently on a bench, we look opposite ways, away from each other, embarrassed by our closeness.

"You're a doctor, aren't you? He's in hospital." She peters out at this point but I have a horrible inkling where this is going. I've thought the same thing; the only difference being I immediately put it out of my head.

"You could just kill him there."

I just start to laugh and she pulls away, as much as is possible. Laughing can be the sign of the insane or even the ludicrous or simply a sound when we have run out of anything to say. A lot of laughing is like this. I'm not laughing because I'm happy or because anything is funny. I'm just laughing because, when every other option has been used up, this is all that's left.

She ignores my laughter. Maria is tough and roughly made and the toughness that I hadn't seen before is becoming increasingly obvious.

"There must be a way of killing him in hospital. People are always dying in hospital."

I laugh again because she is right; there is plenty of death in hospital. It's just that this is different.

"God, Maria, you're asking me to kill someone."

"Yeah."

One thing I like about Maria is that she is so blunt. She lets that yeah sit above us. Then she looks me up and down. It's a strange movement, like she is sizing me up and has a way of making me size myself up. Am I up to this, she is saying?

After she's looked me up and down, which gives me a queer sense of being undressed, she carries on.

"It's easier if he just dies. It's either that or plenty of other people, me included, you included most likely, mestizo kids, girls, men. How many will it take to persuade you?"

So suddenly it's my decision as to whether a whole host of unknown people should die. So maybe, if I grew my thoughts enough I could persuade myself that killing this man would do what is my prime function, to prevent death. Maybe that's not murder at all. It's a sort of preventative medicine for society. I mean some people have to make these tough decisions. It's just that it's not usually me.

So after this little stepwise rhetoric, which is pushing me to make this ethical leap of faith, I feel just how threatened, tired, brutalised my brain has become.

"I'll help you," she is talking to my face now. "I'll show you who he is. You just have to do it. I don't know how, otherwise I would."

She is suddenly animated and her head shakes with an excitement. I look deep in her skin, her eyes and see something new in her that I haven't noticed, not completely. It's a particular type of beauty, a livingness that's stained with life but not defeated by it. Some very unusual feeling comes over me, like there has been a sudden reverse in magnetic poles, that all laws of nature and physics have been temporarily suspended.

When I speak again I tell her I really don't know, because, well, I really don't know. What am I meant to do? Is there a correct or an incorrect answer to this?

There is a lot of silence after this. Maria is good at silence.

It is one of the hottest days of the year today. Kids sit on the roadside kicking tennis balls and bottle tops. It's Caribbean or something like that, and Wormbridge has transformed itself into Kingston or Trinidad. People hang like dogs in the heat. They all turn to look as I drive past; the doctor has met his nemesis.

I used to love days like today. It's just that I'm irritable. I wish I could just climb up Queens Long Down, sit at the top on a blanket, look out over the Severn and write some more crap poetry while I drink some ice cold white wine, and think about colour and shape. There feels to be a hope on hot days, like there is no tomorrow, a lovely shallow transient hope that beauty will ultimately preside and summer will carry on forever. Now I feel as though all hope is gone. Well not entirely. Better to say that hope is running out, like time does.

The Lime trees whisker and wink in the sky as I drive past. The only hope I have left is that, if I can do something, if I can play God for a moment, then the summer might come back to me and I won't be at the mercy of the Brothers, and more particularly

Maria, as I am now.

I question myself incessantly, but really that's nothing new. Sometimes I feel confident that this is the right thing to do. Then like a filmy vision, all that confidence just dissolves. Physically it dissolves and I realise that what I am contemplating is wrong, just wrong and it's only that I'm putting some heroic gloss on this to make it feel right. The scientist in me undone, for good.

So then I feel tired, very, very tired as well as lonely, lonely and hungry and stuck. I've never felt so tired. It's probably just the wine and cigarettes and lack of sleep. For a moment I think maybe it's ME and then I just laugh. It's like some part of me has gone bad and flooded my veins with a sickly poison. My eyes are hurting and it feels as though there are wires around my scalp being ever so subtly tightened as the day goes on.

When I arrive at Severn breakers, I have forgotten that the front doors don't open. Alan comes out of the office to greet me and then has to watch as I clamber into the back seat and out of the back door, like it's some sort of performance but one that takes away all pride.

Alan is in his red overalls. Alan always wears those overalls and I wonder briefly if he has a whole set of them or just one. He says hello and then looks at my car. He has one hand on the back of his head, scratching, and the other on his belly. I keep thinking of Alan as part breakers yard and the breakers yard part Alan. The soil around the huge piles of cars has gone dry and smooth hard. The sun lights up on some old quality chrome bumper and makes a bright star-like thing in my eye.

"Looks like someone don't like you that much."

The way he talks it's almost like he's just thinking, not talking at all, like these are the actual words from within his thoughts, un-translated.

But then I have to agree with him. It does look as though someone doesn't like me.

"You scared?" Alan says.

I nod at him. He jerks with his head that I am to follow him and walks off down one of his avenue of cars, casting narrow shadows as we walk.

"You meant to be scared," he says.

I am not sure whether this is a question or a statement. But I seem to have to say yes, whatever he means.

He leans his head back and scratches his scalp. He pushes his lips out and looks not directly at me but up and to the left. He's about to tell me something, something that is important, something he is reluctant to say.

"Look Dr Bradbury, I've heard some stuff. All I'm saying is that I only just got out from under those boys' noses and it sounds as though you're on the list."

I look at him like I am part of a cartoon and my jaw has just dropped, although I don't think that actually my jaw has moved at all, maybe its just my guts. It is a jolt and I have had too many jolts. Does everyone know my little predicament then?

"Alan, hang on a minute," I say. "What are you saying? What have you heard? I'm on the list for what?'

Then he changes the subject rather quickly and nervously.

"So what model was that car?" he asks, before he clambers, with a surprising agility, up one great pile of cars. I think of mountaineers and whether there'll ever make mountains out of cars and then I notice the silver birch against the hazy sky and its fine lattice of leaves that become animated in the slight breeze. As I watch him climb over this pile of wreckage, I think it's about now that I realise all I have lost: the surety that I had, the last time I came to see Alan, my place in the world. I remember Paul asking me to sign what essentially was his death warrant, just over there by the office. That was the place where I began this descent, which, with a little rewind and a proper bit of doctoring, I could extricate myself from and by now be surfing on a West Wales beach. But then how could I have known? Life is made inevitable by a plethora of tiny decisions, and although none has been particularly wrong they all add up to some huge indictment of me.

Unbelievably he has a Skoda Octavia exactly my model. I think all along he knew this but didn't like to say. I think that maybe it will turn out to be a good day after all. Maybe I'll go to the river and swim and drink that white wine on top of Queens Long Down just like that.

"I'll get them off for you today, it'll take a while and I know you're a busy man."

I tell him briefly that I'm not a very busy man,

how they took my job and I've split with my girlfriend and then her house got burned and the police think it's me.

Alan is wise. He has a face and a voice that make me want to tell him everything. He's the wisest man I know after Claude. When I've blurted out all this stuff, he just looks at me a long time. He doesn't look up or away or anywhere else. He just looks at me.

Then he creases his face up, like he's just about to throw it away, scratches the back of his head and carries on looking.

"Someone really don't like you, do they?" he says, after a bit.

By this time, we are standing back by my wounded car. He looks down at it as though for confirmation and then he nods again and this time scratches the side of his head.

"I got an idea who it might be," he says.

I look at him just in the same way he looks at me. The sun is hot and makes it feel like we are in another world, which we aren't.

"Let's put it this way, shall we. The ones I know like a bit of Sunday worship."

I am a little shocked because I really wouldn't have guessed. Alan is too Wormbridge, or more exactly Ardley to get mixed up in this, this shit, as Maria would have it. He is too wise. He, unlike me, would keep his mouth shut and his head low.

I wait for him to go on, but he doesn't.

"How do you know about this, Alan?" I say and I'm looking at the ground as well, as though we are both studying an insect there.

"My uncle," he says. There seems to be a lot of uncles around here and in general they seem a mixed lot.

I nod and then I keep quiet. You see I am learning; it's just a very slow process, that's all.

The silence is filled with the sounds of roads and summer: insects and cars, wind and tyres.

Alan is still scratching his head, pushing his lips out.

"It's that girl I feel sorry for."

I notice the mottled insignia of a Mercedes: the three pointed star, or is it a circle, and I notice how the bevels of it reflect the light. From a child I always thought of this as a target, a gun sight, and with the silence I feel it line me up, like an eye would.

My tiredness comes back.

There's this unnerving feeling that we aren't alone, not that there is someone near by, but that there is some spirit, some victim that is haunting us, or watching us anyway.

"She never really did much wrong, and then they killed her man. She's wounded, you know, deep down, she's wounded. They did some horrible things to that girl, horrible. No wonder she ended up like she is. But then you know all this, don't you, being a doctor and all that."

I carry on listening; I'm not about to speak now.

"Yeah, I was never that much involved. Uncle who used to run this place, he was well and truly up to his neck. Then, just to complete it all, they chop his head off. Execution. Horrible."

He shakes his head, like he's proving to himself that he's still got his.

You can say a lot of things about Alan. For one thing he doesn't waste anything, most particularly words or cars for that matter. His mind seems cluttered up and strewn with wrecks from his past, but, in addition, there are large clear avenues and he sort of knows where everything is.

The problem is I have no way of knowing, from his expression, how much he does exactly know and it's almost like he doesn't know either, as though he stumbles across facts and memories and finds them as surprising as me. The only thing I know is to keep him talking. And to keep him talking I need to keep not talking. Life is simple, if you let it be. It's not life's fault if it gets complicated and messed up.

The sun carries on its path to the west, across the flatlands, the wetlands, the dirty River Severn, across the Forest and out over the Brecon Beacons. I stand still and lax in the heat hoping that Alan can give me something incontrovertible, something categorical that leaves no room for doubt. What I really want is for Alan to make up my mind for me. Shall I kill him or shall I not? Come to think of it, I suppose this is a bit unfair, but where, anyway, is the fairness. Life isn't fair. Everyone knows that.

Talking has stopped. We are both looking at the ground again. I ask him where he worked before here, although I'm sure he's told me before.

"Bristol Airport," he says.

"And…and you knew Paul did you?"

It's almost painful to carry on.

"Well, in a way, I sold him a door for his Jag."

"Just before he got killed," I say and we both nod.

I know this already and it means nothing. We are going no where and I seem incapable of getting what I want, partly because I'm not clear exactly what I do want.

"Alan, do you know who killed him?"

"What's it to you? How can a doctor get messed up with all this?"

"I'm just worried, it's about the girl really."

He softens slightly. His voice had become sharper. Now it is back to how it was most days: slightly high-pitched but soft, almost melodic.

"I don't know how much you know, see," Alan continues. "I told the missus I wouldn't ever talk about them again. Not ever."

So Alan is married. That's something I didn't know. Not that it makes much difference. Except to Alan I suppose.

"Don't talk about anything if it makes you uncomfortable."

There is a pause as he weighs this up, like he is considering some wreck and what it should cost, or some sort of decision that he is finding difficult. Then he starts talking again.

"They're just dangerous. That's all. They have ears everywhere. Anyway, I hear he's ill, the fucker. Maybe he'll die soon and we can all live in peace."

"So it's just the one man?" I ask.

"There used to be more, but this thing is infested

with nervous people who think the rest are out to get them. It's built on hate and paranoia I suppose. It's like they are a bunch of cockerels and gradually the biggest one won." Then he stops and swallows hard.

"Look, Dr Bradbury, I'm trusting you, because of your profession, and because, I don't know, because you seem to want to help that girl and because your car got beaten up. That's the Brothers who did that. I've seen a lot of that. I just do my best to replace what they destroy. They know I never say anything: I'm too scared to speak. And if you're in with them, I can promise that I've never done or said nothing about you people to anyone and I'll keep everything to myself."

Alan is scared now. He has said too much. He knows he has said too much and I can almost feel his heart beating at about two hundred beats per minute. In a way, though, he has done what I wanted: he has made up my mind, he has answered my question that he didn't realise I was asking.

He carries on talking, "I've never caused any problem, I looked the other way when I needed to. I've never done anything wrong and I've never done anything against the Brothers. I just couldn't carry on at that Airport. Not with the children, not with all the money they were handing out. My nerves got shot; I had to get out. But how can you un-know what you know. That's my problem. If I could take something and it would prove I had forgotten everything, I would pay anything, anything you want."

## Smallpox Hill

He stops for a moment. Alan is always doing this. As though some more alien thoughts have overcome him and blotted out what he is thinking. I am thinking about a pill that makes you forget: re-format yourself like you can a computer, and roll you off again to make another start. I'd have some of that as well. In fact I would be willing to fight Alan for it if there wasn't enough. Strange how we both come to the same conclusions.

Then Alan begins again. "I know you're good Dr Bradbury, I can tell. You're not smart enough to be bad."

I wince a bit. I think this is meant as a compliment, except that I always thought I was smart, before now anyway, so that it feels like he can see, the whole of bloody Wormbridge can see I'm not smart at all.

I tell him that there's no need to worry about me. Well there is a need but not because I might grass on him.

Then he says, "The trouble is, see, things aren't always what they seem around here."

I laugh. Then he laughs. Then, quite spontaneously we hug each other and I realise that I'm right. His heart is going at about two hundred beats a minute and mine isn't far behind.

Cars go past and insects rub their wings together. I am no further on really. He has told me nothing that I didn't know before. Yet there is a hope rearing up. I know that Alan is a proper person, a normal person and it feels as though I haven't met many of them for a while. Then I realise this is why

I love to work in Wormbridge. It's just people like Alan: old fashioned people who like life to be straightforward. Full of proper normal people, full of people that aren't bothered by fame or influence, full of people that just want a normal life.

Then later on I feel like Brutus hugging Caesar, or like St Paul and Judas mixed together.

"Funny, isn't it?" Alan continues. "What's happened is fixed in stone. Nothing can budge it, and then what's going to happen, no one won't ever know, not even if they think they do. That's why we become so anxious, as a rule, because we don't know what is going to happen."

I nod because I know exactly what he means.

Later I think of him saying that. I'm always thinking about what Alan said. It's just that by the time I get to think that, Alan is half way to being dead.

There's no way either of us could know that.

# CHAPTER FIFTEEN

They say you should stick to things you know and there's one place I know like the back of my hand, so to speak, and that's the Royal Hospital.

I even know the telephone number; I've worked there for years. I am feeling a little better than before. I like Alan, I like Alan a lot: he makes me feel better.

For a brief moment it is as though I know where I'm going and in addition, how I'm going to get there. They say sportsmen are relieved to get onto the pitch and I know how they feel, although there is nothing remotely sporty about what I am about to do.

I speak to another nurse this time and yes he has come out of theatre and yes he is OK although he will not be allowed visitors tonight because he is in a high dependency bed. That means more nurses but no relatives and friends, which has its blessings. He is cradled up in the loving arms of the NHS but at least he won't have his weirdos around him.

I mentally and physically prepare myself. I need to be in role, slightly arrogant, busy, no time. If I were in a film I would be described as a sort of Ken Loach non-professional rather than the method actor I want to be. I open my briefcase and take out two thirty milligram vials of Diamorphine: a drug sometimes known as Heroin, invented in my training hospital as a non addictive form of Morphine and about five times as strong. They got the strength bit right at least. I mix it with water for injection in a 10ml syringe and replace the needle guard. That gives me about twelve hours to use it, before it starts to crystallise out. Sixty milligrams should be enough for almost anyone, except if they have a massive habit. I must ask Maria about that.

I smoke about three cigarettes. It's as heavy as hell outside, like the air is laced with some mercury like metal. You can feel the weight of it saddle on your skin.

Then I ring Maria and she doesn't say much, she just says a time. I tell her about the car and she tells me she will drive.

I am virtually twitching by now with a sort of excitement and dread. I smoke and smoke and would dearly love a drink except that I am meant to seem like I'm working and alcohol scents you heavily, like guilt and perfume. I find my old ID badge and another a woman left in my room once when I was on call. She looks nothing like Maria but they so rarely check. I put two stethoscopes in a bag that we will later drape around our necks, some slim book, some scraps of paper, and some pens. I look at my old name badge for some time, Dr Nicholas Bradbury, with a grey background. Then I angrily chuck it in the bin, like Clint Eastwood does at the end of Dirty Harry, but without any charisma because I'm not and never will be Clint Eastwood. I actually want to be no one for a little time. I put my GP pager in my pocket.

Then I have another cigarette. When this is all over, I'm going to quit again. Just now though it feels like it's the only thing calming me down.

I'm just waiting really, sitting in the kitchen with another cigarette, when I hear the tiny squeak of the front gate. Maria would just sit in her car, I think. So I open the back window and creep through it into the back garden that slopes downwards to an open field that, for some reason, is almost blue in the heat. Around the grey Cotswold stone wall I catch a glimpse of one of them. It's Clive. He is wearing a light blue shirt, good quality, and this chavvy jacket with stripes down its arms, something pseudo military. He is nearly bald so that he has three fangs of hair encroaching on his forehead. He is suave but in a horrible way. And in his hand he has a gun, the first gun I've ever seen. It's surprisingly small and black and dull in the light. I can even see his hand feeling it and tracing its contours.

This is the man who does the killings then, and talks to me on the phone. As though to confirm it, I get a peek at a huge shiny black BMW 7 series sitting in the lane outside the house. With all the trimmings.

Oh God, God. This is the moment I've been dreading. The radio will be on and I'll have a shoe off and a needle in my foot before you can do a three-point turn in that car. Or maybe he'll just shoot me, if I put up a fight, and make a horrible mess of my bedroom as well as my head.

I have sometimes been depressed, it's true, and sometimes, very rarely, I've thought about ending it all, sort of like a whimsy, an idle thought. I know now, beyond any doubt, that I really don't want to die, not at all. I love life too much, even the one I've brought upon myself. The consequence of this is that now I'm frightened like I've never been frightened.

I lean back into the window and grab the bag with the stethoscopes and ID and then I vault the back fence into the field. If I am quick I can double back around the old path behind the pub, which I sometimes take at night when the moon is out and I'm feeling that way. I am just an adolescent poet deep down. If I can get to the main road I might be able to head off Maria, and get away.

He must see me at some point because I hear the roar of his car; not for the last time either, and I think he reverses up the lane.

I walk quickly but try not to run. I don't want to arrive on the road just as they do, or run into them accidentally. So I pass through this old brick doorway that used to be the entrance to an orchard, through the pub car park and into the estate of half posh sixties houses with mock Cotswold stone effect and double garages.

I used to dread seeing Maria, waiting in line at the surgery, waiting for her to play her cutting games and her get-as-many-medicines-as-you-can games. Now she seems to me like a salvation: Maria in her big pale Mercedes. She arrives about 5 minutes after the big shiny BMW has roared off down the hill in a great squeal of tyres. A ridiculous way to drive, I think to myself, the tyres will wear down in no time. Maria must have just missed them and I appear from where I'm hiding.

I open the door that I notice does not match the rest of the car. Maria is looking good. I've told her about how she should dress, even down to the pearls, which are probably fake. She has a white shirt, crisp, slightly patterned at the front, a skirt that's about to her knees and tight around the hips. She hasn't taken any shit and her eyes are open and glinting like she is a child and has been waiting for this party a long time. She has washed her hair and cut it. She has a side parting so that hair covers one half of her face. Her complexion is clear and recovered fully from the times when she has cleaned it with a toothbrush. Not even Eminem would know about the cutting. It's as though she's been converted into a middle class person, like some sort of TV makeover, and they've done a good job.

I tell her she looks good and she just nods. Her head wobbles a little as she drives, like she is humming a tune in her head, which I'm pretty sure she isn't. I am feeling awful and I stare out of the window.

She seems to know exactly what to do about getting away from the men in the BMW. She doesn't seem particularly stressed by them as I tell her what happened, she carries on driving slow and sort of solid.

Maria, in fact, drives like an older person. The car, as though it is a borrowed pair of shoes, feels too big for her and swishes backwards and forwards. The hills peter out after Wormbridge. Ardley is entirely flat and alluvial and dotted with houses that are dumb and low slung.

Then she insists that we lie low for a couple of hours, so that it's getting darker. She parks up behind this hedge and we just have to sit and wait. Maria barely says anything for all this time. I want to cry but I know I can't cry, not in front of Maria. It's not how murderers behave, or men for that matter, although I seem to remember that Maria has seen me cry before anyway.

We both smoke incessantly, although it's almost too hot to smoke.

Maria has managed to get me away from the BMW and the man with the three fangs of hair pointing forwards: the ex-friend of the ex-stepfather, from Clive. They must have just got bored and gone back. Now, however, I am in no doubt what they have planned for me.

There is something strange that can happen to you in a short space of time. Both doors are open and Maria and I sit looking out over the Severn Estuary. Flies and birds sing lazy and looping in the heat. The sun has a heady feel of permanence, nostalgia: go-between days, like when we are younger. I try and think what exactly I'm doing. The grass in the field is parched and brown and even the bramble leaves are curling in the heat.

So, lets see. I am sitting in a car with one of my most mad patients, having been chased out of my house and now I am contemplating killing a man in hospital. Questions hang lazily in the late afternoon sunshine. It is only when something is lost do we want it the most, like Rosie, my job, my equilibrium, my sanity maybe. Counting them up I realise what a mess I'm in, numerically, except just about now, in a few minutes, its all about to get a lot worse, so that afterwards I might look back at this moment, with Maria manipulating the pedals of the Mercedes like some small boy doing levers for a train, as she eases the car through the gateway. I might realise that I - at this time - am not in such a bad position and it's just a question of pathos or bathos or whatever the right word is, I'm just wallowing in my misfortune because, perhaps, I like to. Perhaps I like the melancholy and regret. Afterwards, there isn't even any time for that. Pessimism is, after all, a luxury and quite soon I just won't be able to afford it.

So, finally, like we are waiting on the edges of the stage, Maria pulls the Mercedes back onto the road. The darkness is beginning to gather in the corners of the world. The road is empty and Alan's yard on the right is lit in an ultra white unforgiving light. Alan has put up lights around his property because they are deterrents in a way that I do not fully understand.

However the lights tonight just manage to frame a scene that is like some ancient myth. It's strange because I'm sure I've seen this before. I really don't know where.

In the yard, just outside his office, is Alan, still wearing his red overalls. He has no time now to ponder life or scratch the back of his head because two men are pushing both his arms up his back. Next to the office is the black BMW that looks peculiar amongst all the heaps of wrecks. It has lovely bumpers and the shine it has is almost magical. Just as we go past the gateway I see them shove Alan to the floor and as he falls I get a glimpse of his face. It is almost purple and contorted with fear. This is maybe why it feels like an ancient mythological scene. There is something about killing in cold blood; it's sort of Greek and malign and ageless.

Maria accelerates away by pressing the accelerator, like she is putting out a cigarette, tiptoe.

"Maria," I say (it's a naming because, I don't know, perhaps I really mean this for once), "Maria, we just can't leave this to happen."

She stops the car and glares at me. There are moments of silence.

"So, what do you want to do, tough guy?"

When Maria sneers, God does she sneer, like her face becomes full of hatred and exudes a sort of poison, like a secretion.

"Going to take them on, syringe to syringe, are

you?" Then she laughs a ghastly un-Maria like laugh; an inhuman laugh like perhaps she might be losing it. Another desperate un funny laugh.

I look at her and she looks at me and I wonder what game she is playing now. At least she has stopped the car.

I think briefly that the reason that Maria has survived as long as she has is due to utter selfishness, something that I really can't blame her for, given the circumstances.

So I get out of the car. For a moment I feel dizzy like I'm going to faint. Along the road back to Alan's gateway there is the stench of some out of date road kill and the discarded rubbish of other drivers.

As I turn into his yard, into the orange white of his lights, I suddenly realise I have no plan; I really don't know what I'm going to do. A medium height out of shape doctor with a loaded syringe in his pocket is not exactly a threat. They are kicking Alan, who is trying to put up a struggle that's clearly infuriating the two men. They, for their part are trying to drag him inside to his office and I'm pretty sure what will happen once he is there. Then I look at the BMW and, although I've never known much about cars, I'm thinking that car could really bomb it, given half a chance.

I wish I could just concentrate. I wish my mind would behave for a moment or two. It keeps becoming tangential and obtuse like it's had enough and would prefer to be somewhere else instead.

But I've decided I like Alan, I really like Alan. So

I just go ahead, the fool that I am. I shout Alan's name.

There is a brief pause to the violence as, one by one the three of them turn and look at me. I look back at them.

To a greater extent, I feel like this is my defining moment: my Bay of Pigs, my 9.11, my battle of Britain. Because, lets face it, I'm not going to be a great Prime Minister, or scientist or win a Nobel Prize and make some speech that the whole world is going to pour over and admire. I'm not going to discover the vaccine for smallpox and save millions of people from a horrible death. There is just this one man who I have grown to like, a good man with no ulterior motives. I'm just small scale and this is my moment, with three men looking at me, and insects making white lines around the lights.

They let go of Alan's arms, kick him one last time, and then launch into a sort of run, a fat persons run. I see Alan struggle not towards his office but towards the mountain of cars. There is blood on his overall, well I think it's blood but, since the overall is red, it could be anything: sweat, vomit, tears or a spilt drink. I can see that he is going to find a place to hide, in amongst the mortuary of cars, the chaos of all that is stacked up and rotting, in the knowledge that only he really knows his way around.

I begin to go backwards, watching them coming towards me. I see Clive reach into his pocket and I remember his little short squat gun that he flaunted around at my place. Then I turn and leg it out of the gate. One shot goes off but it thuds into the tree across the road. My God, this is Wormbridge, not Los Angeles. What on earth is happening

Unlike myself, Maria knows exactly what I'm doing. She has reversed the car so that it's just next to the gate. I run and as I open the door - the door that doesn't match and looks particularly wrong in this light - I see two things: first Maria ramming the gear stick into first, and second the swish of headlights behind us, like a lighthouse, turning in the gateway.

For a big fat old car, this Mercedes can really move. For once in its life it gets to use all 2.3 litres of its engine. There is no physical sensation that compares with travelling, moving quickly. It is precarious and hot headed, a thrill. The only problem is I'm just not sure it's enough to outpace a very shiny BMW 7 series.

At the A38 she turns unexpectedly towards Bristol and away from The Royal Hospital. I am sweating and confused and swear at her and ask her where she's going. She looks at me like she can't work out whether I'm joking, and it's not very funny, or if I am completely stupid.

"Sometimes you just don't get it, do you?" she says after a moment. By now Maria is clocking about 100mph but still the distance between us and the halogen white of the sinister headlights behind, seems to be getting closer. The villages we roar through are sleeping dormitory villages that sit like small plastic beads on a cheap old necklace.

There are often Police down here with their

speed guns. Maybe they will stop and arrest us and then we won't have to play this game anymore.

Now however, there are no Police waiting to pull us over. There are only the white headlights behind us for company and they are getting nearer. The pits in the road shake the lights, like they are eyes hanging on wire.

"So are we just giving up?" I say to Maria.

"Does it look like I'm giving up?"

I can tell she is angry because she lapses into a type of 'you are stupid' rhetoric when she's angry. I know rather too many of this woman's moods for my own good.

There is silence apart from the roar of the engine, but I'm better at silences now. Maria has taught me about silence. I can remain calm and say nothing for hours. Perhaps if they ever did bother to torture me, I would be good at that too; hold onto my secrets and keep my mouth shut.

It's all getting intolerable and I'm sweating and I'm coming to hate Maria and the jaundiced way she is treating me, when something unexpected happens. The headlights behind fall away into a layby and then I see red lights as the car turns and heads back.

I start shouting and then I look over at Maria and she, for all her barbed comments, is smiling, sort of grinning. It's a good moment. I bang the dashboard in adulation of the Mercedes. Maria turns left and gets onto the M5, heading north. I'm thinking that if she goes for it, we will be at The Royal before the BMW.

## CHAPTER SIXTEEN

The M5 is empty. The sky shines its last purple shards behind tired looking willows, trying to last out the summer, and the odd crumbling farm houses. To the right is Herdsley Peak, Queens Long Down, Smallpox and the hills around Wormbridge. It's like I've been taken out of my world and I'm being allowed to look back into it, like it's enclosed in a Perspex box.

I smoke out of the window and so does Maria.

She looks over at me, "You're not going to fuck this up are you? You seem nervous as shit."

"I am nervous, Maria, and no I'm not going to fuck this up."

Maria doesn't seem convinced. She does her well-known sneer at me: the top lip curling upward and miserable and also malevolent and intolerant.

"This is your bit, this is," she goes on, "I thought you would know how to do this."

"I do, I do. It's just...oh God.... no one has ever tried to shoot me. That's all." It's my way of showing her that I'm not playing games. She doesn't look very impressed.

I then decide, irrevocably, that I will never, ever allow myself to get this involved.

Maria remains an enigma, a complex difficult person. I think of Alan, how he said she was damaged, that was the word he used, but he is only partly right. She is strong, is Maria: if she does something, she does it hard. Yet she is obscured, to me at any rate, behind everything that happens to her. What she is actually like, I realise, I have no idea. There is a warm genuine affection within her, a hardness, a manipulative side and a complete hopelessness as well. Perhaps that's what he thinks damaged means. Or maybe, being in the damage industry he just uses the word sloppy and quick. Like when I say someone is sick, it can mean anything.

So here we are driving through the dingy light industrial units that surround The hospital, like a shallow rank tidal lagoon would surround an island. It's nearly dark, but at this time of year, it's never completely dark. The sky has this feeling like it's reeling from the heat of the day like a watch with luminous hands, or that some of the intense light is left in reflection to fill the sky from beneath: a planetarium or a big fish tank.

She swings the big lumbering car into the chaotic car park of the hospital at the foot of what used to be known as the tower block. Up above, lights are like a liner: an illuminated cliff rising up from its more human dimensions to something huge and out of scale. The front entrance is lit like a jewellers shop, a cheap one like Ratners, if they still exist.

The air outside crackles nearly, like cellophane. Rows of patients in pyjamas stand outside and smoke, standing in their slippers. The light is harsh and shiny. Maria has on her name badge. Her pearls don't look cheap either in this light. I remember suddenly that she has come into some money. I ask her if they're real, and she nods. She fingers them between her index finger and thumb.

I just want this to be over now. I've had enough and I want to be walking around outside and not have all this filling up my thoughts.

As we walk past, one of the smokers leans his head back and blows smoke into the air, like he's breathing on a cold night. Except it isn't cold.

A security man is checking ID on the front door. Fuck, I say to myself and then I feel giddiness come over me again, but this time more like vertigo. Maria looks up at me, and I look away because I don't want her to see my face. They lock the other entrances at night but they don't usually check ID.

There I was thinking that this part, at least, would be straightforward and then they do this. A thought within me starts to stir that maybe everyone really knows, knows what is inside me, or that there is a controller who is putting obstacles in my way, tasks to be overcome and frankly, I wish he would stop because what I'm trying to do is difficult enough already.

I do not generally do panic, but I do it now. I feel like I'm walking to the edge of a stage: the lights are on me and I can't see anything beyond the end of the stage, all is black. I've no idea if anyone is watching or not, but, nevertheless I feel watched.

I'm really not sure if I can blag this ID business feeling like I do. Apparently there has been some baby taken from the baby unit, and in typical hospital fashion, they get sort of heavy afterwards. At this point I'm not sure if my nerve will hold; I might just burst.

I look back as we stand in the queue. The night sky above the hospital is the mauve of a cushion. Ringed like a halo by the neon surrounding it, the cathedral stands up tall and gaunt. Car parks, like seas, lap the edge of the hospital grounds. I realise this has gone too far. I want to go now, leave, and disappear like a weakling. I'd like to be a weakling; I've no problems with that. I've been pretending, playing some good killdeer and now I just want to stop playing.

This is the problem: I'm not sure whether this is totally the right thing to do, or totally wrong and the more involved I get, the muckier and more confusing it feels. I've taken this Diamorphine, I'm about to lie past the security men, there'll be cameras; in the end I'll be caught. The deceit has gone on long enough.

Maria tugs my arm and we move up the steps towards the security man. I put my hands in my pocket and wait. There I feel the bleep and I immediately become someone else again. I must keep myself from changing so rapidly. The bleep, of course, the puppet string of my life, the way people keep me on my leash. I turn it easily to arrest mode and the thing screams. I grab Maria's arm and rush for the door. I keep my face down and say excuse me, the way a doctor does. I mutter ward 16 and the security man - and here is the elegant bit - helps to remove people from my path.

We rush through the foyer that is decked in vile green plastic ribbing, is it called, and the horrible textured wallpaper that looks as though it should be carpet. There is the hospital smell of canteen and forgotten corners. Past the jewellery light of the front door I turn my bleep off again. We are surrounded by this ghastly atrium: a place where people congregate, a public space where none of the public feels in any way relaxed. The lift block is to one side and there are plenty of people waiting: people in their theatre green gowns, doctors in white coats, nurses in blue or white or green, patients, looking about as healthy as the doctors. That lift area always had a cosmopolitan feel, like a college or a shopping centre.

We stand to one side and wait for an empty enough lift; I'm not walking those 5 floors.

As we wait, I start talking to Maria. She nods and she leans her head closer as I talk. I see the strip light above us reflect slightly on her nose. I see three empty corridors stretching away from us, their tiles reflecting the same bands of strip light.

We are saying nothing really, something about cancer and operations that means nothing, but we are talking. We step into the lift and fall silent. No one is really looking at us. It's easy to be anonymous in anywhere this big. It's why people like cities in the first place. No one knows what you're doing and no one cares.

The ward lies ahead of us out of the lift. I touch the syringe in my pocket, like it is my amulet, which, I suppose, it is. My only weapon, as though I've never realised that knowledge is a weapon before.

I am jumpy but as well I feel a flood of something within me, like there is a pending release.

The ward is empty enough. The nurses are having handover, which means they are gossiping about patients and staff. They sit noisily in conference. The light clusters around their station like a load of waving hands.

The ward is arranged so that each bay has four beds; these lie to the left as we walk down the long gloomy unloved corridor. Parked up are unused beds, drip stands, blood pressure machines that have their blue cuffs hanging wantonly like the sting hanging beneath a jelly fish. The clutter in the corridor reminds me of Severn wreckers: the forgotten left over detritus of life.

It's busy and other doctors are walking, floating around like ships. Each bay we come to Maria checks and shakes her head. He is bound to be close to the nurses' station because he has just had a major operation and they'll want to keep an eye on him. He is in a high dependency bed after all. It's just a shame he didn't die under the anaesthetic. There is always a rude health around evil people.

## Smallpox Hill

There is no one much watching, because this is the most terrifying part for me. I want to be anonymous and I suppose transparent really. I think of life stretching out and summary justice. Then I think of how I am taking advantage of the fact I know death; I know how it comes about. I know death from nearly every side. I am prostituting my skills, my knowledge, and somehow I've managed to mangle my position; my morality into thinking this is OK.

It is important that we are not seen clearly. Each bay is full but we still haven't found him. Like an open door that we need to pass through in the night, we grit our teeth and walk past the nurses in their conference. One looks up momentarily, so I mutter something to Maria about Haematology and she nods. Their voices are behind us. I finger the syringe full of Diamorphine that's about to be slipped into the vein, up and into the heart, up to the lungs, back to the heart, up into the neck to the brain where it will slowly stifle the desire to breathe, stifle the desire for anything.

My only desire is to have this over with. I was imagining the ward half deserted maybe one sleepy sister propping up her own chin and dreaming of the next tin of Quality Street. Instead it feels like half the nurses in the world have decided to work here tonight.

I know which is the man as soon as I see him, just from doing those searches on the computer. Although he is nothing like that picture, I know it is him instantly.

In reality he is grey with smooth skin, oddly handsome and pure looking, like someone's grandfather.

Maria tugs my arm. I've been waiting for this moment for so long. He is in the first bay after the nurses' station. The lights are dimmed and there is a night-time hush that I have always hated.

There are two nurses around him, fiddling with all sorts of kit that surrounds him. He is barely awake, his eyes three quarters shut like Maria's always used to be.

Why is there always something in the way, some barrier? Why is life this complicated?

Then I remember what Alan said once: if life seems simple you probably just don't understand what's happening.

We walk further down the ward and then come back, but they are still there. So, in the end, we leave but this time by the back stairs. I'm desperately in need of a cigarette, so we go to the Doctors' mess area, where I know you can smoke out on the top balcony. Both of us drag so hard that the red slug of lit tobacco is big and ugly in the night. We don't say anything. There doesn't seem anything more to say.

Then I say, "You can wait here if you want. I know who it is now."

"What, and miss the fucker dying?" She fires back at me. She's always so sharp, so protective of herself.

"That's the only bit I want to see. I want to see him dead."

I raise my eyebrows, resigned.

We are walking back; the corridors are virtually empty now: long lonely places with nowhere to hide from the saturation light. At the lifts, we stand and wait. There are others here, waiting as well. They speak quietly. One man, on his own, is mouthing words, like he is practicing his lines. His trousers are too short for him and he has an intense look in his eye, like he is desperately holding something back.

The lift will not come, it seems like it is bouncing around like a ping-pong ball between G and 1. People are beginning to stare at this man, with so intense a look, stare at his muttering. For a horrible moment I believe it is the man who wears the robes, the satin, the man that I hit. He has that same disengaged look.

Then he comes up to us and I realise it isn't him. He opens his mouth to speak and to start with nothing comes out, as though he is frozen, petrified like a fossil on the bottom of an ocean. Time keeps doing this to me: lasting forever in a moment. Then he opens his mouth and pours out the filthiest diatribe.

"Doctor," he says, "Doctor, you are the evil one. And this here, next to you, this is Lucifer herself, the most beautiful of the angels, thrown from heaven because she was despicable."

He is salivating and trips over his words, like they are water particles in a hose pipe having just been turned on to full pressure. He comes up really close to me, the white of his eyes are both yellow and red. I can smell his horrible teeth.

Then he steps away, "Here," he announces to the watching crowd, pointing at me, "here is the killer in our midst, here is the dark angel, he is the man who has forsaken the lord."

I try and move away from him but he grabs me with a hard feverish grip.

"He is trying to escape, look how he tries to hide from me, the all seeing one."

The rest of the crowd start to shift anxiously, as they should with me being abused in this way.

I shout that someone needs to call the mental health unit; someone rushes off. He still has hold of me.

"Tell me doctor, have you not killed, are you not planning to kill, are you not a killer. Can you renounce the devil in you? Can you repent unto the Lord?"

I have always found it's better not to say anything to these people, but it takes all the self-control of good killdeer to avoid it.

He turns on Maria, "The devil herself. I can see through you, you evil one. Have you not heard that Jesus died on the cross for your sins?"

"Shut up!" Maria says quietly.

"You would deny me the lord? You would have me as St Paul? I shall not stop from saying his name."

He grabs hold of her but she reacts angrily and pushes him away, so that he trips on his overlong slippers and falls. Some people standing around us start to laugh.

When he stands up again, it is as though his

mania has been cranked up. I, on top of my nerves, can barely take this. His eyes are diseased and bulging like they are about to burst.

He begins to shout, at the top of his voice. Some nurses and a porter from the ward next to the lift come out. The porter is a small man, but he walks straight up to the man and grabs him. He is strangely docile to this man's touch and the porter leads him away down another of the long corridors.

I am shaking with a repressed horror. Maria is furious and dark, like someone has insulted her mother, except that as far as I know that wouldn't bother her.

I motion to the back stairs. I'm losing myself here and I need time, time to be ready.

The walk up the stairs is long and banal. The smooth polished concrete and the metal handrails, painted in a gloss red.

I'm not superstitious and I'm not easily spooked, but this man has got to me. Like all horror, it is merely the suggestion of the thing, not the truth of it all but the suggestion, and for about the fifth time I wish I hadn't come to The Royal Hospital.

# CHAPTER SEVENTEEN

I put my hand in my pocket and there is the syringe, at least four hours old now.

It will have to be now. There is no other time to do it.

The ward is quieter than it was; there is still a gaggle of nurses around the lit station area, but this time we don't need to get past them. There is a dim light that suffuses his bed, and the brighter lights of the different machines and alarms around him.

This is when I suddenly become what I wanted to be. Cool is the wrong word for this. Ruthless is better, like steel has suddenly slipped into me, and a mounting hatred, not based on what this man has done to Maria and thousands of other children but because of what he has done to me. How he has turned me into this, this killing machine, this murderer. I suddenly hate him more than I hate Justin Whatmore, or the man that watches me, or

Sue or anyone else that I can't quite think of. Is this what happens to murderers? Do they ramp up their hatred so that they can do it, actually kill?

I pick up the drug chart, wrapped in its blue folder. Maria stands next to me. He, as I suspected, is on a whole cocktail of drugs and in addition has a morphine syringe driver. I look around and see two nurses walking towards us.

Fuck, fuck, fuck I say under my breath. I'd forgotten that this could happen. I am sweating now and nearly shaking. The nights of poor sleep are rattling around like they need somewhere to lie down in me. And there isn't anywhere.

Instinct can lure us or it can guide us and at this moment I do the one thing that will save us. It's simple really; just like playing another game.

I re-hang his drug chart on his bed and move onto the next bed. It's walking away from where I want to be, so that no one comes sniffing around. Doctors are allowed to be arrogant and antisocial. I don't even look at the nurses and for all I know they don't look at me. I've been a doctor long enough now to be a complete natural. I flick the next patient's drug chart off the foot of their bed and leaf through it. Maria, because she is an expert player, realises immediately the elegance of what I am doing and puts her head near mine so that I can smell her shampoo.

"Fucking assholes," I say, and she looks up at me and at this moment she smiles, almost like we are lovers, like we have secrets, special secrets. It gladdens me more than I can imagine. After all, I'm only really trying to keep everyone happy, most of all myself. It's just that this man has got in the way of that, and I am about to swot him, fly like. Then these people get in the way.

"I want him to see my face as he dies," Maria says.

I don't understand her or quite what this means to her. Instinct tells me that this is the most important thing she has ever done in her life, but I never actually get her to tell me this. It's like psychotherapy on a grand homicidal scale. I've known Maria so long now and I've always wondered how I could help her, help her properly. I've a very strong feeling that this will help her properly.

The nurses are quickly gone and we have stared at this complete stranger in the next bed for long enough. There are always complete strangers wandering around hospitals. It's a dangerous place to be, in hospital.

We move back to the bed and I again pick up the chart. Forty-five milligrams of Diamorphine is going into him over twenty-four hours, the slow drip of the syringe driver. That's one thing at least. He can't be an addict if that's enough to keep him this drowsy. Maria was right about that.

He starts to move when he sees Maria and his eyes light up at first before he realises that she shouldn't be here and there's this look on her face like this isn't a relative visit and there's no flowers or fruit that she's bringing. He looks at the white coat and then he looks at me. He is pathetic really. He tries a smile but it comes over as just pure fabrication, he tries to sneer at us and look cross or deadly but this is even more laughable. This poor man has just had half his guts chopped out and he's in no state to do anything, least of all hate. Hating takes up so much energy and he simply hasn't got enough to do it.

He is obviously rich and influential, you can see from his hands and his pyjamas. Otherwise he's just another piece of meat waiting in a hospital bed, in the loving arms of the NHS.

Maria puts her hand under the sheet and I see her squeeze his nipple in her hand and then rotate it about five hundred degrees. You can see he is in pain even though he's been coshed with all these opiates. Then she reaches down to his testicles and grips them as hard as she can. He again screams but its all silent, it's like a quiet mutter. His blood pressure is going up, so I turn off the machine, and the alarm attached.

I tell Maria to stop it. She again smiles at me but this is not a good smile, not like the one she just gave me. This is the smile of a sadist, the smile of hatred. Smiles can be the best way of showing hatred.

I pull the syringe from my pocket and then I realise there is no need to use it. The driver is fully loaded, that was probably what the nurses were doing before when we went to smoke. It had, if the doses were right, at least twice as much, probably four times as much as we needed to kill him, if it all went in at once, instead of over twenty-four hours as it should.

I unhook the rubber that holds the syringe in place, and turn off its alarm as well. Thank god its not one of those new ones district nurses use with the lock on them. Then I push the plunger fast so that the clear liquid bubbles slightly as it goes into his vein. It goes in so easily. It's so easy to kill people in hospital, a slight slip of the thumb and that's it.

It seems for a moment that this must be too easy and that it won't work. I re-engage the syringe driver and make sure the setting hasn't changed. Then I watch him.

I think slowly of the molecules invented a hundred years ago, rushing up his arm, around his heart to his lungs back to his heart and then to his brain, where these same molecules will cling to some vital piece of his hypothalamus and he will drift into death.

It's probably too good for him to die from this fantastic human invention. Someone once said that only the good should die in their sleep. Anyway, I'm quickly realising there is very little in the way of justice to this life business. And the only bit of justice I'm concerned with is to stop this man breathing.

So I watch and Maria watches. I often feel at work that I wish I had a magic wand. It's a common, rather trite thing for a GP to feel, like there is nothing I can do and doesn't any one else realise that, but still sometimes I wish I could pick up a pen and wave it while saying some incantation, and all the problems like loneliness and loss and sadness might be cured. I remember this as Maria and I watch this man, this ill man. It's like I've done my spell and we're waiting for it to take effect. Slowly, it begins, his face loses its colour like some plug has been pulled and he's breathing slows and then stops. I have watched people dying before and it fascinates me. After about two minutes, the quality of their flesh changes. Maybe it's at that time that their soul leaves, if things like souls exist, which I personally have no idea about. The flesh becomes firmer and waxier; it crosses over the skin, this change, like a cloud over a deep green valley.

I feel briefly for his neck pulse, which unsurprisingly isn't there. I miss a few things as a doctor but I'm pretty good at telling when someone has died. It's not complicated. Not usually.

Anyway, he's dead. There is no doubt. Death is categorical like that.

We walk away from him, having propped him like he is still alive.

The back staircase is cooler than the ward. There is a feeling of ecstasy, a release, like I have finally burst and all the pressure has gone. I skip down the stairs and Maria is close by me.

"It seems so easy just to die," Maria says.

I answer vaguely. Sometimes it seems miraculous, when you learn about the human body, miraculous that we manage to stay living at all. Life is delicate and fragile and yet within it's confines there can be so much suffering. When really we should be grateful to just be alive, like I feel now, it seems sort of pointless to get miserable. But I know these are rash and unheralded thoughts and that death is just something that I specialise in.

The back stairs lead out into the horrible green foyer with the smell of canteens. As we step into the garish and unforgiving jewellery shop light, I feel Maria freeze next to me. She turns towards me and unexpectedly hugs me and presses her body hard into mine. But it's not affection this. She is not offering herself to me, she is shaking and playing some other weird game, God knows what this time. Then she slowly eases me back into the stairwell, where we have just come from. The door has long pastels of glass on one side and as the door closes she looks out quickly through these.

"What the fuck are they doing here?" She points to two men standing looking up at the signing of the wards. It's the two men who have probably trashed my house and ruined my CD collection, having already done some work on my car. They have tried it on with Alan and now they are back to see the boss. Clive is still wearing the nasty jacket with stripes down the arms. It looks as though they have just got passed security. They look bothered and bad tempered and not people that you might share a joke with.

We watch, like we are stuck in a cupboard. Because they are not expecting to see anyone they know dressed as a doctor, they are just not looking. I wonder how they managed to blag their way past the security, except that these men have friends all over the place. And why did they take so long to get here?

We need to get out and they are hanging around

and talking quietly to each other. Sooner or later, the nurses are going to find him dead, find the empty syringe driver and they may put out some sort of alert. We have to be out of this by then, we have to be in the anonymity of our landscape by then, well away from this cheap jewellery shop. The two men seem aware of this, as though they are standing sentinel, as though they are aware of what has happened. Except they are too late: the man they have come to protect is dead in his bed. And the thing about death is that there are no second chances. You can't redo a scene and become undead. It has something that's missing from the rest of life. It is categorical and certain and you can only do it once.

It's about five minutes that they wait. Then a third man joins them. Maria opens her eyes wide at the sight of him. They quickly move on, and disappear from our narrowed view of the foyer.

I never find out who this third man is, but Maria is clearly surprised to see him. She mutters something about the Cromwell Road, but there is no time for questions and quite frankly I really don't care. I don't care anymore.

I open the door and check that they are gone. We head for the main entrance and are quickly out, our faces are down and quite suddenly we are in the Mercedes and we both light cigarettes simultaneously. The night sky is royal in colour and makes you want to rest your head on it. The horizons are still light in the north. Tomorrow I'm thinking that I'll spend the whole day lying in the sun next to the river. I'll have beer for breakfast like a Brazilian and spend money on some sumptuous lunch from William's Kitchen. I'll buy myself anything I fancy, and I'll buy Rosie some flowers and try and win her back from her Mum and the cool clutches of Justin. I can do anything now. Anything is possible.

Maria however has different plans.

"It's going to get heavy around here, the next few weeks. We should disappear." Maria says.

"I thought you said this would stop all the killing, Maria, that's why I did it."

The car seeps through the dimmed neon of the Bristol Road. There is a massive traffic jam caused by some road works and some very slow traffic lights. They must have got stuck in this whereas we had come up the motorway route, the long way round. There are drinkers sitting outside some rough looking pub and the neon from the old match factory. England's Glory it says.

"It *will* stop, don't you worry. It's just that sometimes it's better not to remind them what your face looks like, then they'll forget you."

Back on the M5 I can just make out Queens Long Down and the lights of Wormbridge.

"I'm going down to Cornwall. You want to come?"

I often think recently that life is split into eighteen-year cycles: eighteen, thirty-six, fifty-four, seventy-two. The four stages of life, like the parts of a book, or the quarters of a football game, the acts of a play, the phases of the moon. Each age has its epiphany moments: its tragedies, its losses, its loves, its wasted moments and times of good fortune. I feel like this is the end of one of those parts, even though I'm only thirty-four. I suppose the ages aren't exact, its not an exact theory, like relativity, after all. I'm not sure quite why I feel this but I do. Life, after all, is just an epic soap opera, where we, the actors, have no idea what the scriptwriters have in store for us. All we know is how long our contracts last. Then the Dr Craigs' of this world take over our roles, and then everyone forgets us and our brief tenure, our short moments of being in the centre of things, when, paradoxically, we feel irreplaceable. No one is irreplaceable and secondly, we only see the world from our own viewpoint and can't truly imagine anything else. So life is a constant surprise.

I remember hearing an actor talking about working with an avant guard director. When the actors started, there was no script. Only a story which was told to them a bit at a time. They noticed, he said, that each actor had a different length of contract. Sometimes one month, two months or up to six months. All those with shorter contracts were told just before a scene was shot, that they were to be killed, and no one else knew, so that there was genuine shock on the faces of the remaining actors, and therefore the film was fresher and more livid. Now it felt like my life had become like that, and I was frankly sick of all those surprises. And on top of that, my life needed a few more jokes, because so far, it certainly wasn't a comedy.

The lights of Wormbridge are beckoning me. For

the first time I seriously doubt Maria. I just want to go home and forget this has all happened. I want to be someone else. Everything feels it has become a game, a ghastly game that we are all playing, and I've never liked games. What can I do now? How can I stop playing? Where can I hide? When you've gone this far from what you know, when you have what the US military call mission drift, you sometimes forget what you are trying to do. I feel a sort of hopelessness fill me. I feel the weight of what I've done sitting on me like that mercury in the air, I feel it slip into me. Later I will look back at this moment as the beginning and also as the end. My insect life moving through one of its instars. And I'm not even acting.

But now I just resign myself to the inevitableness.

"OK, lets go to Cornwall," I say and I light another cigarette.

She pulls the car into the lay-by just after McDonalds, takes the cigarette out of my mouth stretches up and kisses me long and hard and soft and wet on the lips. I notice vaguely that her feet have left the floor of the car in her attempt to reach me. I don't know why I notice that.

Then she begins driving again.

I put the lighter back in my pocket and there I feel the syringe, unused and branding me. I chuck it out the window and watch out the back as it spins chaotically over the hard shoulder. Maybe some lucky junky will find it and have the time of his life. All drugs supplied free by the NHS.

## Smallpox Hill

My lungs hurt and I decide that I must give up smoking. It's going to kill me if I don't.

## CHAPTER EIGHTEEN

It is early November. It is cold. There are hallelujah colours in the trees and the threads of cobwebs strung out over the broken earth catch the light and are like fine strands of silver. I have just had my haircut and the wind sings bitterly in my ears, around my ears. I like how short it is and how the wind makes it bristle pleasingly. Half a centimetre or so: a number two. It suits me that convict look. After all I am guilty.

This morning is important chiefly for two reasons. It isn't the haircut either. I have a parcel that I open just before I leave the house. Inside is a book. It's a very old gnarled copy of The Sound of Music, with a picture of Julie Andrews as Maria on the front, in the Austrian Alps, singing her heart out. Inside, the pages are cut out and there is £10,000 in £50 pound notes. It even looks like a lot of money, and the notes are a beautiful salmon pink. This is one reason. Now I'm not rich and ten thousand is a lot of money.

I walk to the village. The second reason is that the morning is so beautiful; the stained glass colours and the sky being blue like a drop of purest copper sulphate solution, the blue it gets only when it's biting and cold. Copper sulphate is important to me but I won't bore you with why. The thought of ten thousand goes round in my head like a rotating fan on a hot day, even though it is cold. Swishing. It makes you sing, that sort of money and even in my rotten, awful old heart there are vestiges still left of an excitement instead of the constant drone of dread that has filled it so lately.

I haven't seen Maria since she left me to find my own way home from Cornwall. That is the sort of thanks I get. The only thing is, Maria is right. I had doubted her, I had doubted that it would all stop, and after I got back home, well, nothing happened. My car got repaired, Alan came up trumps at Severn wreckers down on the old Bristol Road. He had been found by his wife hidden behind a stack of cars slowly bleeding to death, terrified to move or come out in case Clive was waiting for him. He had needed some emergency surgery down in Bristol following a deep abdominal wound but he recovered quickly enough. There were no phone calls, no one wanted me to die. In fact the three men we saw at the hospital were put away for murder, though they always denied it. A nurse swore under oath that she saw them tampering with the syringe driver. Memories are reliable like this.

Sometimes it feels like I have just made it all up. It was me that was damaged. The trouble is I just can't get myself out of this hole. I drink too much and I am still smoking.

Sometimes I think of Will Self and his quantity theory of insanity. Maybe Maria managed through some trick to transfer her damage onto me. This is how it feels. Psychologist would say transference, but then who listens to them anyway. I have lost my hope and lost my will.

It is constantly surprising to me what exactly cheers me up and for some reason this ten thousand pounds has had an effect. I haven't worked for four months now and ten thousand pounds buys you into plenty of unnecessary things.

I walk down to the village shop.

It's when I'm walking that I see him again. He is wandering up the street, which is called The Street because it's the only street in the village. He is walking, first on the other side and then, just ahead of me, he crosses over the road and walks straight towards me. He is nervous but then why shouldn't he be. I have, at an earlier stage, broken his nose. He wears a long brown coat with a collar like a mane. It reminds me of one my grandma used to wear. Somehow top heavy or, more accurately, collar heavy. I suppose he is about my age. There is no way of telling, no teeth to count, or rings. He is tall and walks by shuffling a little, slightly angular, sideways as though there is a crab somewhere tucked into his family tree. You notice his eyes, his nervous dark eyes that flash shyly, unsure of himself and a little jumpy. Beneath his coat he still has on the majorette type uniform of faded velvet.

He comes right up to me. His hands are stained

from trees and soil. I don't particularly want to stop, but he gives me absolutely no choice.

"How are things?" he says.

Just like that. Just like he knows me. Which in a sense he does. The amount of time he's spent watching. The odd thing is he is about the one part of what happened that makes me feel awful, truly awful.

The wind comes up again and my ears feel shrill and exposed. It is opposite the antique shop whose owner looks sidelong at us as he polishes the top of the unsold bureau. I don't really want to waste any words. That's how I am accustomed to thinking, except I haven't a clue what a wasted word is.

"Oh, OK I suppose."

I am not very enthusiastic. I make as if to step round him. The antique shop owner stops polishing and watches us.

Then he says, "I know."

I stop trying to walk round him. I stop altogether. I feel cartoonish and ever so slightly nauseous. I gag on the moment as though it has caught me unawares, which it has.

"How do you know?"

"I wrote it down," he said.

"You wrote it down?" I have a feeling that my eyes are moving closer together. Incredulous. "You wrote it down?"

For a time there is silence between us. I now also have an awareness that I'm repeating what he says, as a question, for no obvious reason.

"Anyway," I say, "who are you? I've seen you around, watching me and I don't know who you are. Did you work for them?"

He ignores my question.

"So, you work round here?" I ask.

"You could say."

What does this mean? He seems to enjoy this gentle agitation, this infuriating vagueness, but at the same time he is nervous. Nervous like he doesn't know what I'm asking him. He pulls his lip up and sideways again. I am half convinced it is meant to be a smile. But it isn't because it sort of falls down as well, un-smile like.

"So, you work round here?" I repeat.

He nods.

"But you don't work for The Brothers?"

I am being categorical and he hates me being categorical, I can tell. The only thing is it's about bloody time that someone is categorical around here. I've had enough; I've had my doubts and my demons. I want something concrete. A straight answer.

I never manage to get one, not even much later.

"No, I'm just staying here."

"Where?"

"Do you want to see?" he adds after a long pause.

"What, where you live?"

"No, not where I live, what I write down, that is what I mean."

For the first time he becomes a little impatient.

I have to say that right from the beginning I have never trusted this man: it is his tall top-heavy stoop and the unsteady way he moves. At first I thought him damaged in some way like Maria, like me I

## Smallpox Hill

suppose. Is everyone damaged if you look close enough?

For whatever reason, I go with him in the end. Apart from his damaged part there is also something seductive in the way he talks. The words are so few but within them I almost straightaway become transfixed. Also he is harmless, he is thin and slightly wheezy when he speaks and I know he is harmless.

The autumn hangs down over our heads. I look upwards and I can see the sun hanging eastwards and southwards like a cold bright moon while the trees cling on grimly to their leaves. They have golden rod and cochineal. Thirty-four autumns I have seen and each year it catches me like I've never seen it before.

I walk behind him up Limcombe Hill and I become irritated by the very way he walks and talks. Could he not walk straight and stop spitting out his words like they were made of letters and not just saliva. It is a long way round the Hill and then we cut left. The path quickly becomes a Holloway, which is a sunken bridleway with steep sides, like a canyon. I have stopped trying to talk. It is easier to just let him talk when he wants to.

At one point he turns around and says: "You will get to know me soon enough." Then he carries on walking.

At another he turns and thinks of saying something and then decides not to.

Then he smiles at me and says, "Don't listen to everything I say," and he squeezes my arm warmly.

The Holloway gets deeper, like Charlton Heston

passing through the red sea in The Ten Commandments. That's one of my favourite films but you probably don't want to know that. It's the Technicolor I love. Not Charlton Heston and his ridiculous Moses beard.

High up above the Holloway on the right a tree is rooted to the bank. It is a beech and the soil about the roots had been eroded away to leave a canopy above a mysterious area, surrounded by old bulbous roots, four of them, like Doric columns surrounding a Greek temple holding the tree up above them. It's possible to walk right under the colossal trunk. It is like something Gaudi might have created in Parc Guell.

Under the roots sit a gilded chair, dowdy yet fine. The knuckles and gnarls of wood seep a shiny substance like a pearly light. He has some blankets in one corner, which look as though they are his bed.

The first thought I have is that he is mad. It is the gilded chair and the way he walks. Mad I say to myself and begin to feel scared. But very quickly I see that he isn't mad. Well, possibly not. There is something indefinable and unnamable about him that is faintly magnificent, like some proud but ageing hippie who still owns the Sgt. Pepper suits. He sits in his chair and sighs deeply and without reserve. Mad is another word I use rather glibly, I sling it out in an undefined way.

"There's nowhere for you to sit, I am afraid. But then again I suppose that you have not come to sit."

I am, when he comes to mention it, not at all sure why I have come at all. I have ten thousand pounds spinning in my head and bulging in my pocket and I am under a tree speaking to an odd man sitting in a scruffy gilded chair.

"You have come to read of course."

He slowly produces an old tin from his pocket and rolls himself a cigarette. He hands it to me and I roll one to. We smoke in silence. I don't want to smoke really but now I am smoking. We all have double lives and double standards but I am one of the worst.

The way he smokes is like Rosie used to: the index finger hooked over the top of the cigarette, a couple of short puffs to spruce it up, and then a long hard draw. He smiles after the first proper drag, smiles in a way that, although crooked, I begin to like a little.

I ask him about his book. He looks at me in the faint glow and shakes his head.

"You have not yet learned to wait. Only if you wait will the truth become visible."

I must admit that he does have a point. I can't wait for anything: sex, money, answers; I have a problem with waiting. I really don't know why I came or what I'm doing with this man, but then life isn't as simple as knowing what you're doing.

His top lip again drifts up and to the left. Perhaps he is damaged, I begin thinking, properly damaged, brain damaged, like poor Bernard but in a much stranger way. He hands me an old ledger, black with red corners. I try and leaf through the book he has handed me. It has hair like writing crammed together closely and some dates, in roman numerals. The book itself, the writing, is all completely illegible, unless it's a very strange short hand or a whole new script, an alphabet of which I am not aware. Some are arranged like poems, in small blurts of words. The script is wonderful to look at but I cant read a single word of what is written. Its spidery nature makes it seem like a beautiful design, like something William Morris might print for wallpaper, but abstract and without sense, like music.

I look at him and see him looking.

After some time he says, "Do you know what this means?"

"Well….." I say, and then I feel unsure about how to proceed. I just had a feeling that this man might tell me what has really happened. Somehow interpret what I have done, bring some moral sense to it. Then I begin thinking that, in the end, we are all hopeless at mind games; we always give away our weaknesses without fail. In my tawdry and confused state, I have pinned some sort of importance to this man, the mystery within him, and now I have just shown that I am weakness itself and my moral compass is spinning wildly, and more than anything, I am wrong, I have done a terrible thing. There is no other way of looking at myself. I have shown him that I am guilty.

He is smoking another cigarette. He inhales deeply on his roll-up, and sighs. It's not really for me that sigh; it's for everyone and himself, and no one as well.

"Had enough yet?"

"What on earth are you trying to do to me?" I shout, and whether it's the six months of hell, or a

## Smallpox Hill

deep rooted frustration in my life, the words come out like a yell, a howl of anger and pain.

"Do you think that by shouting and screaming the past will somehow cease to exist?"

I look him up and down. It seems as though he is deliberately obtuse and obscure. He doesn't fully make sense. I take some long deep breaths and manage to bring back a feeling of calm. There is a long silence.

"So, are you or were you working for the Brothers?" I ask him.

He looks at me that way, curious, half slung, ugly and then he begins shaking his head.

"I really don't know what you are talking about."

"You seem to know everything else about me. You see, I always thought you were working for them. It's the way you watch me all the time. It's horrible to be watched."

"I am sorry."

"It's me that should say sorry. I must have hurt you."

He makes another expression that I don't fully recognize. A sort of shrug but within it something more complex as well: something like that is the past; it is not relevant, and also an affirmation that yes, I did hurt him.

"I just thought it was you who watched me walking up to Rosie's house, who saw me running down the hill with Maria. I thought you were spying for The Brothers."

"Who are The Brothers?" He asks, like he is from a foreign country.

'They're...they're a bunch of evil men who kill

and…"

"But who are they?"

He looks me long in the eye, as though I am an insect and he has speared me onto a show board. I begin to squirm inwardly as though now I am trying to escape.

"I don't really know their names. One is called Norman, I think. "

"Then why are you so worried about them?"

"Because they tried to kill me."

"When?"

I stop. I don't really know what to say. It's not like me to not know what to say. "They threatened me. On the phone. They came to my house."

He nods his head but it is clear he doesn't really agree with me. I rub the edge of my index finger up and down with my thumb. "Anyway, it's horrible to be watched liked that."

"Yes," he says in the most annoying way of his, like he doesn't really mean it. "We know always what we have done. We can pretend to others and even ourselves that we haven't done anything. This doesn't change what we have done."

Silence comes between us.

"So you have never heard of The Brothers?" I say after a minute or so.

He says no and shakes his head. Then he continues. "But perhaps you have done the right thing." He smiles his crooked smile, the lip pulling away from the teeth and heading up and to the left. Then he touches me gently on the arm.

"It's time you went. It has been good to talk."

"Yes," I say.

## Smallpox Hill

For most of the time I'm wondering what this man is really like. I am trying to unpick him, find out about him, and he is just remaining awkward and unclear. Except now he does something quite strange. He touches a little grey sap that has appeared on the gnarled knots under the roots and then anoints his head solemnly with it. He then turns to me and grits his teeth and then give me a full smile, before muttering things under his breath. It dawns on me. He is completely mad, mad in a true technical sense. I feel like he has been talking about real things, quite profound things, until I realize that he hasn't. He is just beyond sense, mad, as in, he ought to be in Fairmead, which he probably has been, at some point, anyway. I feel a strange comfort in his madness, for when the rules of sense and logic have gone, at least we don't have to whittle away to find the truth. It is like playing the ultimate card, the joker, the ace of spades that make all other considerations worthless.

I shake his hand and then, I don't know why, I lean forward and hug him. I'm not sure if it matters anyway. Then I turn away and walk down the little Holloway with the beech trees magnificent and full of hallelujah above me. It feels as if I am walking under the parted waters of the red sea. I turn back to wave and he smiles at me, with just the left side of his mouth.

I'm not sure exactly why, but meeting this man has put me in a good mood. Or maybe that's just the effect of having ten thousand pounds sitting in your pocket. I decide I will walk to Wormbridge and put this money in the bank. The truth of the matter is I'm desperate for money and desperate to have people around me. It can be a lonely life being a doctor, but it's much lonelier being a nobody, being nothing. I even tried, a couple of month before, to hitch back up with Louise and restart our careless love, but after a couple of times it just felt wrong, in some strange way, too careless and without meaning. In another way, all the fuss with the alibi and the Police I think scared her, spooked her as hunting people would say. Instead of being a somewhat enviable catch I had become both a no one and a liability. I began to feel what it was like to be outside society. In fact, at times these last few months I've felt that my whole body is empty, as though they've opened me up and cleaned me out so that I am just a shell, with no real substance, an exoskeleton. I have always been alone, all my life. It's only that these last few months I have felt people cower away from me.

As I walk, the trees flag me like I am an important person and this is my parade. There are long dark damp stems and then the stained glass colour, the yellows the oranges, making the sky into a huge cathedral window. Someone once said that it was the sugar in the leaves that brought out this colour. I think about all those people that have died because their sugar was taken from their blood, I think that perhaps its sugar that is the most important thing in life, the dictator of death and beauty. I then think that this is complete rubbish and I laugh, I laugh at myself for such ridiculous thoughts, the thoughts of a man who has spent too long with himself. In my minds eye there comes a vision of the molecular model of glucose, and for some reason I laugh again. Out loud, on my own.

Is this a sign of madness?

I'm not sure if it's the ten thousand quid or meeting the strange man but I feel better. I have been ill for so long I had forgotten what it was like to feel as light as this, almost weightless so that the wind, if there was any, which thankfully there isn't, if the wind blew it might take me up into the trees and drop me down somewhere else.

There is a rope swing half way to Wormbridge, where the bank of the hill is steep, so that you slip from the ground and swing out to an almost impossible height. I have three or four goes. The valley of Wormbridge is laid out below me, the houses in their crescents, the small windows of bedrooms. Then there is Smallpox out to the right. I marvel at how different Smallpox Hill can look from different angles, as though it is a different hill. From here it looks castle like with its steep sides and its buttress trees.

The hedges down Drake Lane have lost some of their vibrancy and with that their shape. The beech trees that circle the hills around are clinging onto the autumn as though they have some vested interest in it going on forever. I am walking through Wormbridge and for the first time since I got involved in all this Maria nonsense, I feel a sense of hope and freedom, like I am at last recovering from some long degenerative illness and my muscles are flexing for the first time.

There is the sullen man who rescues the trolleys

from all across Wormbridge and rows them up at Sainsburys. There are the two cheerful women in the new health food store. There is the always-empty fishing tackle shop and the fourth charity shop selling used children's toys. There is Barclays Bank, its sky blue logo and its horrendous front elevation, the Old Ram with some drinkers lined up like wooden ducks along the bar. The woman from The Hard Yards has just locked up and is skipping, like she does, on her way home.

I'm outside the fourth charity bookshop when to my surprise I see Maria; she's about three yards away. I haven't seen her coming up. She looks good, does Maria, she's all up together; her shirt sleeves are rolled up and all those horrendous scars have healed well and left only tiny thin lines on her smooth skin, like a pale lattice work you might see in a carved Iranian window. Life has this way of healing in an almost miraculous way, if you can wait long enough. That's what I've always loved about being a doctor. You're working with the most extraordinary and beautiful machine. It makes life, for me, so much easier. All we need, mostly, is the time to heal.

I have to say that I'm shocked to see Maria. I haven't seen her since Cornwall. I didn't even know she was still in Wormbridge. And then there she is about three yards away.

I smile and do those sort of headshake things when it's all slightly embarrassing. Because of all this I'm not really at my most observant and I curse myself later for that. She smiles and, although she doesn't often smile, when Maria does smile, it seems so fresh and natural.

She has one arm hitched through the arm of her companion who I briefly look at. He is not really very tall and not really very short either, he is not really anything. I think for a moment that he looks remarkably similar to Paul and then my mind starts thinking on as it does, about how we all tend to repeat things all through our lives and how everything can replay itself as tragedy and farce, or is it the other way round. By the time I've been through all this they have passed and my legs have carried me to under the Queen Ann town hall that is rested on stone pillars and has a market area underneath.

I suddenly stop, as though my brain moves at the speed of a dinosaurs' and has just detected some painful stimuli that has occurred ten seconds before.

Then I decide I'll chase them back up the street. There are very few people about in Wormbridge.

Then I start to doubt everything. We cannot live unless we trust something about us. Perhaps I have really lost the plot. The trouble with being completely mad is that you have no idea that you are. There is no one to tell you and anyway, you won't believe them even if they do.

You see, here is the trouble. Reality and the truth have a way of warping themselves so that we start to see the world how we want it. And even if it's the wrong interpretation, our minds do everything in their power to justify our view.

So here I am, running like a weirdo up the High Street of Wormbridge, a place I have decided to dedicate my life, chasing after a couple who have caused me a whole summer of torment, who have nearly capsized my whole life. But by the time I get to the other end, there is no one to be seen. There is only a picture of some friendly ethnic pharmacist smiling and inviting you into the chemist shop. The autumn wind blows dust and crisp wrappers up into an unspectacular vortex that steadies itself briefly and then blows down May Lane leaving a stream of discarded detritus in its wake. It feels like there is nothing left but the cruel wind blowing dust into my eyes, behaving in a way that is scurrilous and neglectful.

Maria and Paul are nowhere to be seen.

# CHAPTER NINETEEN

In chaos theory, miraculous things can happen just by chance. Throw the cards high enough and they may come down as a royal flush, or sometimes just as a pack of jokers.

How can this be Paul. Paul is dead. I certified him dead. And now I see him walking around Wormbridge with Maria. There are certain tenets of reality that are being challenged here and my poor traumatised mind is on the brink of collapse.

I feel like a man with fully fledged Tourette's syndrome, I run up and down the streets with about fifty emotions running through my head and no doubt, if you examined me about fifty different facial expressions as well. I read an article by a man who nearly drowned and he described how truly, his life flashed before his eyes. Apparently, when faced with absolute death, our brains have the facility to sift through all our memories and desperately search for one that might ensure survival. I realise mine is doing exactly this, sifting through hundreds of yards of my life to try and work out how possibly this could be Paul.

First I think that, in a confused way, he was never Paul, but was another man playing Paul. Why, though, be someone else when you can just be yourself. We aren't in a play after all, but life itself. It makes no sense at all.

Most of the time, we are trying to make something coherent out of chaos, we strive bitterly and pedantically to make all the elements fit a story. Our minds constantly search for the narrative in the real world. So that's what I'm trying to do as I stare down the street. I am trying to process and ram all the facts that I know into a format that makes sense. And it won't work, it doesn't fit.

I walk back up the street, past O'Sullivan's the ironmongers who now have a rather thin looking garden bench on special offer together with some empty hanging baskets with a price label that is luminous orange and shows brightly even though the shop is in deep November shade. I am peering into every window I can, past The Hard Yards, The Valley Building Society with its mock Dickensian front that frankly I have always hated. Where did they go? Did I even see them at all. I rub my newly shaved head.

There's another narrative going on within me that is saying this is all me. You see, I am constantly wrong, I have been and always will be because I don't concentrate at the right times. So, if this really is Paul, then who did I certify up in Paul's room, because that person was definitely dead. I'm sure about that. I'm good at spotting the truly dead. That is when my head spins again, and I literally have to lean against the railing outside the old bank building.

Paul, or whoever the body belonged to, was facing the wall, and because of the young testosterone filled police detective boy, I never really rolled him on his back. I had to lean over him, stare in his eye with the torch. I saw his eyes and I saw his feet and I saw the back of his head but I never really saw him all at the same time. I didn't link up his separate anatomy. So, I'm thinking, if that wasn't Paul, firstly, who was it, and secondly who killed him and then, if we extrapolate further who really was that man in hospital that I killed.

So this is why I'm leaning against the railings of the bank. I have had the most elaborate killdeer manoeuvre pulled on me. I spool it out in my head and reshuffle the already dog eaten cards that I hold in a mess in my hand. It can't have been Clive who killed Paul, for he would have realised it wasn't Paul. Unless Clive himself was in with these two, which from personal experience even crazy people would rightly doubt.

It is horrible when you lose all faith, when all that you know, you doubt. Some people say bereavement is like that, some say it the beginning of the disintegration of the personality. I'm not really sure about anything. I have murdered a man just because Maria wanted me to. I think for a long time about this, partly about what an elegant game she had played, partly about how I could be so wrong, so utterly wrong. This is something else that happens within us; we abhor being wrong and so try and change the rules so that we are right. Cognitive dissonance it's called. You see how much learning I have. Not that it has ever helped me much. I believed in her, I was wrong and there is no other way to look at it. I cant dissonance my way out of this one.

Like a dying man scanning his life, I think of Maria screaming at me in her house and the little piece of lace draped over his face and the hysterical reaction and her calmness afterwards. As always with Maria, given the hand she has been dealt, she had made pretty good use of it. Then, as my mind races on, like it does, I remember some physicist talking about a pack of cards and how there were more combinations and sequences of fifty two cards than there were atoms in the universe. For some reason I think of these myriad possibilities and stop thinking about Paul as clearly as I should.

These thoughts are going through me and I'm supporting myself on the railings outside the old bank. I feel as if all is lost. The money in my pocket suddenly seems like horrible toxic money, killing money. They have made an unlikely hit man out of me. I truly feel all my guts have been taken away, I am left empty.

A hand comes on my shoulder and then a familiar voice.

"Great to see you again Doc."

I look around and Paul grins up at me, with that array of disorganised teeth and the slightly menacing and beautiful lips. I realise one thing, even though I have been so thoroughly done by these people. I like Paul, I'm glad Paul isn't dead. I realise that we make these snap judgements about people, and perhaps it is a chemical reaction or something similar to chemistry that happens with emotions. For no really good reason, I like him. He didn't deserve to die, as far as I know; he seems like a good person, or at least he did seem like a good person, before I had thought it all through. Anyway, I forgive him the Doc business.

"Paul," I say, " I can't believe its you. You alright?"

"Yeah, I'm fine, it was you we were worrying about."

I had forgotten how fast he talked and how he ran his words together. Wewereworryingabout, that's one word. As he says this, he turns a little further to where Maria is standing. She, for her part, looks fantastic. She is quite tall and now has become elegant in the way she holds herself. Her eyes are open, she smiles and she has always had a beautiful mouth, although this is congruent with the rest of her beauty. She doesn't come over all triumphant, she looks concerned. Concerned about me. That's when you know that you're at a low ebb, a really low ebb. It's when someone like Maria is concerned about you.

"Looks like you need a cup of tea, Dr Bradbury."

"That's about exactly what I need." I say. Paul smiles in his crooked grin.

The three of us enter the little low café, about half way along the street, run by a couple of young women and decorated inside in those weird whirls of plaster, artex swirls and lacquered chairs that are slightly greasy to the touch. It's always friendly in here. We sit in one corner so that we can watch the street. Paul pays for the teas and we sit down in a triangle.

"So," I say, "you've got a bit of explaining to do." They both laugh and Paul pats my hand. "In fact," I say, "the last time I saw you, you were dead." And they laugh again. It does seem strange how these two have transformed themselves. They are light, airy and full of a new confidence. They aren't worried or paranoid any more. They are happy, they both look really happy.

I think for a moment about the quality of paranoia and how the mind can make things in you, and that suspicion is created somewhere deep in the brain matter. I think of all the times I felt watched, watched by The Brothers.

"I suppose I was," Paul says ironically. Having been dead for some time, I am fascinated by Paul now he is alive again, giving me another unexpected opportunity to look at him carefully. He is rough looking, tanned but not glamorous, and I wonder how he manages to look both kind and menacing at the same time. It's partly because I'm sure his face is slightly lopsided, he has a shaved head, a single stud earring and these lips that are unusually beautiful, like an elegant lady might have.

"And here you are, not dead" I say. It sounds rather stupid and I realise it is rather stupid

"It's complicated," Paul continues. "We never properly thought it through. We just found him dead. The rest came from that."

"What, arranging for me to kill someone for

you?"

"No, you saved our bacon, Doc."

I look down at the table and stir my tea. My fingers seem suddenly short and ugly and I begin thinking how clumsy I am.

"I'm really not sure what I've done, with you being alive now. I was just trying to help, I think...." My words tail off and I begin thinking about all our subconscious acts and how we forget most of them and don't realise the tiny effects we have on the lives of others and where those ripples may end up. So as I stagger through life in this clumsy way of mine I wonder what other howlers I have made.

"No, no. Don't be down hearted." Maria says. "You may feel like a fool now but you just didn't know how perfect you were."

She waves her hand as though she is dismissing something. It's the first time she has said anything, but she smiles at me. Her eyes are open and she is smiling. "I couldn't tell you because sometimes you are just a bit unreliable. You would have probably just gone to the Police and us two would be dead at the end of a needle before the week was out."

"So, let me get this straight." I say, after a pause. "You kill someone who looks quite similar to Paul, pretend it's Paul, Paul disappears, you collect your money. So how come The Brothers didn't know. Surely Clive would know as he does all the killing."

"Hang on doc, you are getting well ahead of yourself here. Who says Clive does all the killing?"

I have this very strong sensation of peeling an onion and having to discard each layer and somehow, too, my eyes are stinging as I realise that each layer is wrong.

"What," I pause and then almost stutter over the words " so.., so it was you two, you killed them, you killed the junky, you killed Julian, you killed whoever that body was in your house."

"I've never killed anyone, Doc, and that's the honest truth, and Maria here just had a hand in that one you killed, you know, at the hospital. So you can't come over all accusatory, you were the only one of us that's done some killing."

Paul reveals this slightly hard side of himself like a flourish of a cape, and then he smiles and says to Maria, "He really didn't know, did he." Maria nods. I'm not sure if I don't catch a smallest piece of edginess in that nod, for, despite the mystery, I actually know Maria rather well, and I detect a slight discomfort, a scent, which doesn't last more than a fleeting moment.

"So The Brothers think they've killed me except they don't know that I'm not staying in that room any more."

"So that's brave," I say. "You allow someone else to die on your behalf."

I'm feeling slightly angry because these two seem to be getting off scot free here, leaving me as the only evil one, which is only partly true. And when I'm angry, I get sarcastic, like I'm some tough cop, like Clint Eastwood, except in truth I have nothing to back up my toughness with, so that it appears just rather whiney and petty.

Paul, to give him credit, does not react to my barb. "They send Julian in to do the killing. I've never met Julian, see. They send him to kill me, because I knew what was up and was refusing any more trips to Chaipas. They didn't know about the new loser who is renting out my room, seeing as I was sharing Maria's." Paul grins that slightly misshaped smile at me, almost a smile of complicity, and also slightly unpleasant.

"This bloke is asleep most of the time, stoned out of his head. He probably didn't even notice he was dead." Paul laughs at this but neither myself and Maria do and it falls slightly flat.

"So Julian kills him when we're out, we come back and notice he doesn't appear down stairs at 4 ish when he usually totters down to the co-op for his fags and whatever else, so we check his room, and there he is, facing the wall, dead. We have a dead body in my room. By then I already know what's going to happen to me. I've applied for life insurance, so they were clearly thinking that they had killed me. That's, as you know, how it all worked."

"So I called the police," Maria continues, "and Paul here made a run for it. They came and said we had to get a doctor, and that's when it could have all gone wrong. Why on earth did it have to be you. Aren't there other doctors in this town? You knew Paul, I just sat there waiting for all the shit to arrive, when you announced that it wasn't Paul who was dead, it was another man. But you never did. You just obsessed with shoelaces. We thought, maybe you were on to it, we didn't know. It was a terrible time."

I realise that they weren't even playing any

clever game or anything, they were simply reacting to each card as it was dealt. I begin thinking of conjurers, and how the sleight of hand, in reality, is to make you concentrate on one thing, while the deceit is being played out at another spot where you aren't even looking.

"So what happened about the junky who was killed instead of you. Did no one miss him."

"No one knew anything about him. That's the thing Doc, some of these people just live underneath, or up out of the way, in some place where they are just left to rot away and die. No one wants these people around. No one is looking out for them. He had become a no one. A non-person. The rest of the world pretend they don't exist. There isn't any family, friends, anything. The only two that knew about him was us."

I think about this for a little and drink my tea. Paul puts his hand in his jacket pocket and pulls out an apple. I stare at it for reasons I can't immediately remember. It is mostly green with a streak of cricket ball red down one side. He bites into it with his large teeth. I watch him chew and swallow, almost as though I am hypnotised. He watches me watching him.

"I suppose you would say all of this, wouldn't you." I say morosely when I have come to myself. I feel so mixed up and complicated inside I genuinely don't know whether to be happy or sad about sitting in a café with the recently bereaved Maria and her once dead husband.

"You can believe what you want," Maria continues. "haven't you noticed how quiet it's become around here." She looks over at Paul and I look around the café, with its tables and empty chairs and out into the street where there is almost no one about. I killed that man, and maybe it was the best thing, except I don't really know, I don't know anything anymore. Not with any sort of certainty. I don't know firstly whether it was truly wrong to kill him and secondly, whether I entirely trust these two. I am confused on a number of different levels.

So here is my dilemma. Philosophically it is wrong to kill. I had talked it through with Claude who knows about these things. I trust Claude and I had to tell someone. He told me that this is the simple deontological position and it makes life simple. Rules are rules, like the laws governing particles or the predictable effects of gravity. The problem though in philosophy is that there is another argument, the teleological view that says actions can only be judged by their consequences and looking at myself from this position, perhaps I am not wrong at all. I flop from one extreme to another

So I say, "Is that what this is for," I slap the roll of cash down on the table. "Payment for killing?"

"Look we couldn't decide about this." Maria says. "We have loads of money now. The Brothers certainly knew how to set up life assurance. And we knew you had been suspended from your job and the whole thing had fucked your life up and we just thought you deserved it. But you don't have to keep it, not if you don't want to."

"I really just want my job back, and I've got an

interview next week."

"Yeah, that was me, I sent the health authority and that medical council a few letters, saying how you had helped me, and that all those dead bodies around you had been explained by the arrest of Clive. I said you were a good doctor and had been unfairly suspended. I got a few other to write as well. Everyone likes you Dr Bradbury. You're a good doctor."

"Whatever that means" I say even more morosely.

"Don't be so hard on yourself. You probably saved my life as well as Paul's. Isn't that what you're meant to be doing. "

"Yes, but not like this. I'm meant to cure disease, not kill murderers, and I don't even really know if he was a murderer, maybe he was just someone you didn't like."

"You don't know the half of what that man has done. He is truly a monster. I nearly told you once, in the surgery, but then I got cold feet. Do you want me to go into details."

I just shake my head and for some moments none of us say anything.

My tea has gone cold by now, and so Paul gets up and buys me another, along with a bacon roll for himself.

Then we move to the table outside, on the street, with all the passersby looking cold and weary already, with the start of winter. We, all three of us, smoke and then I decide something. This is going to be my last fag, that's enough and I need to change. So I really enjoy inhaling deeply, while Maria and

Paul do the same. We talk about Wormbridge and Smallpox Hill, and then about the Mercedes and I tell them I love that car and Paul says I can have it for £2000, and then I say, it cant be worth that, and he shows his dark underbelly a little by gunning hard for a good price. He tells me those 230's will be worth a fortune one day. I say I'll think about it. At that moment Bernard shows up and sits and smokes with us. He looks better as well, in some ways his face is angelic, so smooth and clear, like one of those female portraits by Modigliani; a lovely almond shaped face of youth. He has a job down at the furniture factory, where his lack of speaking doesn't really matter. He's taken the room where all the killing took place, but he says he doesn't mind, it's a nice room with a view out to Smallpox Hill. We talk about the ghastly orange colour of the wallpapers and he tells me they painted it a month ago. Just white, nothing fancy.

As we sit at the table, the conversation runs more easily and Paul is laughing in such a vivid way it makes me begin to smile as well. I have these moments when I feel like I rise out of my body and look at myself from above and as I look down, we seem like friends the four of us, talking and smoking and I see my life in a different aperture. I can hear myself talking to them and joking with them. I can see, from this position above us all, that we are just ordinary people living along with ourselves. Then I think with a jolt that looking down on myself is most likely a psychiatric symptom as well and I try and bring myself back to the pavement where we are sitting.

Finally, I get up and then everyone stands up. I say to Paul, "I'm glad you're still alive," and he gives me a big bear of a hug and slaps me repeatedly on the back. Doc, he keeps calling me doc, and strangely, do you know, I'm beginning to like it. It's possible to change what you think. It just takes some mental willpower. Then Maria hugs me as well and then holds me off by my shoulders and stares deep, deep into my eyes.

There is an awkward pause. I smile at her and squeeze her arms. I shake hands with Bernard and then I leave them. I wave back at them from 5 yards and then, just outside The Hard Yards in fact, I look round again and they are still watching me and I do this little slightly embarrassing wave and then immediately regret it. I never had much style to me.

I walk up the hill that leads out of Wormbridge, towards the Oak pub where I was last seen in a Madonna outfit, and then I think of Rosie. Rosie, I miss Rosie more than anything else in my life. I heard that she has another boyfriend now, an artist from Bristol, not Marcus thank god, and the last Claude saw of her she seemed happy enough. I didn't really know what I had with Rosie, and now I do know what I had and now I haven't got it anymore.

I carry on walking around the edge of Limcombe Hill and begin the steep wave like descent toward the Bristol Road, I need to visit Alan to see whether he's managed to finish off the repair to my not very lovely Skoda Octavia. There was a wing mirror still hanging and a small dent in the front wing that needed hammering out. I'm not that excited about

## Smallpox Hill

the car but I'm excited about seeing Alan.

As I walk, I try and get my thoughts straight about what happened and whether Paul and Maria are telling the truth. And if they are, does that make it better. I sit down in the field below the tree line. The sky is clear apart from some cartoonish clouds that look like horses on a carousel and move quickly from west to east. I lie on my back, and in a peculiar way the sky itself and the earth are visibly round if I look directly upwards. I realise at this point that I may never know everything completely.

With that clear in my head, I feel the wad of notes sitting in my pocket. I come to a decision that I will give this to Alan. In some ways Alan was my salvation and moreover he is always short of money, and most of all I like Alan, I really like Alan. He epitomises everything good about Wormbridge. He is honest, hard working and most of all he isn't pretending or playing games, he is who he is and seems to like himself and everyone else. He doesn't want fame and fortune, otherwise he would have got rid of that breakers yard and made some decent money. But he likes that yard. It suits him and he suits it. I don't want that money and he has lived through years of hell because of Norman Waye. It's my way of compensating him for being stabbed; an un-official criminal compensation payment. I feel that he had risked all by helping me and trusting me with his secrets and he nearly paid the ultimate price for siding with me and not just shunning me. So I'll walk down and give it to him.

There you see, that's categorical. I get money for stopping people dying, not from killing. It's a simple rule.

Its just that, well, the world of people is never simple, or for that matter, neither do they adhere to many rules, for individuals and their psychology do not follow absolute laws, we are not particles and we are not particularly affected by gravity, and so it can get very complicated and quite often by the end, we are no less certain about people than we are at the beginning.

So I walk along the big steep hill that slopes towards Alan's down on the Bristol Road and I am feeling better than I have felt for years. I feel like I have learnt some lesson, not really in a clear way, like this is right or this is wrong, but something much more important. As a doctor, you can't afford to lose your energy for caring. It doesn't much matter what you know. Knowledge is the easy bit. It's the caring that is important. Perhaps I had lost a bit of that compassion. For, although I have done something wrong, it was for the right reason. I did truly care for Maria. So now I'm walking down the hill, with trees and hills everywhere and I'm humming that tune to myself, thinking of hills and the landscape being alive with a melody and a narrative that we live alongside and all I can think about is Maria and Julie Andrews and that bloody film, The Sound of Music.

So this is where life leads us.

Smallpox Hill

# ACKNOWLEDGMENTS

I hadn't realised how much time and commitment it takes to write a book. There are many people who have made this possible. I am grateful to Jake for inadvertently spurring me on to finish and his philosophical insights, and to Martha for providing the painting from which the front cover is taken. Writing is really about your readers and I would like to thank Mark and Carolyn Bradley for early and sympathetic advice. Duff Hart–Davis provided invaluable insight and feedback and I am grateful for the time he has spent and his inside knowledge of the publishing world. Special thanks goes to Tim Ingram who has spent hours turning my horrible grammar and spelling into something acceptable and for his many suggestions and my sister Lucy who also helped tidying the text. Abby Conway has been absolutely fantastic in arranging the text and designing the front cover and this book would not exist without her. Above all my thanks go to Rachel who provided many of the themes for this book without even knowing it, for all our long walks and constant discussions and companionship that have sustained me.

Made in the USA
Columbia, SC
20 September 2018